SINGLE,

....

CAREFREE,

....

MELLOW

....

SINGLE,
CAREFREE,
MELLOW

Stories

Katherine Heiny

FOURTH ESTATE • *London*

Fourth Estate
An imprint of HarperCollins*Publishers*
1 London Bridge Street
London SE1 9GF
www.4thestate.co.uk

First published in Great Britain by Fourth Estate in 2015
First published in the United States by Alfred A. Knopf,
a division of Random House LLC in 2015

1

Grateful acknowledgment is made to the following for permission to reprint
previously published material: 'Once Was Love', music and lyrics by
Ingrid Michaelson. Courtesy of Cabin 24 Records © 2009.

Selected stories in this work were previously published in the following: 'The Dive Bar' in
the *Saranac Review*; 'How to Give the Wrong Impression' in *The New Yorker*; 'Single, Carefree,
Mellow' in the *Chariton Review*; 'Blue Heron Bridge' in *Narrative*; 'That Dance You Do'
in the *Saranac Review*; 'Dark Matter' in the *Greensboro Review*; 'Cranberry Relish' in the
Chicago Quarterly Review; 'Thoughts of a Bridesmaid' in the *Nebraska Review*; 'The Rhett Butlers'
in *The Atlantic*; 'Grendel's Mother' in the *Alaska Quarterly Review*; 'Andorra' in *Ploughshares*.

A catalogue record for this book is available from the British Library

ISBN 978-0-00-810555-6

Printed and bound in Spain by Rodesa

MIX
Paper from
responsible sources
FSC® C007454

FSC™ is a non-profit international organisation established to promote the responsible
management of the world's forests. Products carrying the FSC label are independently certified
to assure consumers that they come from forests that are managed to meet the social, economic
and ecological needs of present and future generations, and other controlled sources.

Find out more about HarperCollins and the environment at
www.harpercollins.co.uk/green

TO MY MOTHER,

for more reasons than I can count

And you don't feel you could love me
But I feel you could.

—Paul Simon

Contents

SINGLE,

·····························

CAREFREE,

·····························

MELLOW

·····························

THE DIVE BAR

So picture Sasha innocently sitting alone in her apartment on a hot summer afternoon and the phone rings. She answers and a woman says, "This is Anne."

"Who?" says Sasha.

"I think you know," Anne says.

"Well, I don't." Sasha is not trying to be difficult. She honestly doesn't know. She is trying to think of possible Annes whose voices she should recognize. Is it someone she missed an appointment with? Is this the owner of that camera she found in a cab last month and kept—

"I'm Carson's wife," Anne says.

Sasha says, "Oh!" And even if she sat around from now until eternity saying *Oh!* every few seconds, she would never be able to inject it with as many layers of significance and wonder again.

"I was thinking we ought to have a drink," Anne says. And to paraphrase Dr. Seuss, Sasha does not know quite what to say. Should she meet her for drinks? Now what *should* she do? Well, what would *you* do if your married lover's wife asked *you*?

After the phone call, Sasha finds she is too agitated to stay in the apartment, so she calls her roommate, Monique, at work.

Monique is just leaving, so they decide that Sasha will walk down Broadway from 106th Street and Monique will walk up Broadway from Thirty-sixth, and they will have a drink in whichever establishment they happen to meet in front of.

Because Sasha is anxious, she walks faster than Monique and they end up meeting in front of a Taco Tico on Sixty-fourth Street, but they cheat slightly and go into an Irish bar next door.

"Wow," says Monique when Sasha tells her about Anne's phone call. "That must have been so humiliating for her when you didn't recognize her name."

Sasha frowns slightly. Isn't Monique supposed to be on her side about this? Besides, it wasn't that she'd forgotten Anne's name, it was that Carson never used it. Always he said *my wife. I have to go, my wife is expecting me. Let me call my wife and tell her I'll be late.*

"And how did she know *your* name?" Monique asks.

"I guess Carson told her that when he told her about me," Sasha says.

"So when are you meeting her?"

"Next Wednesday."

Monique looks startled. "That's a long way away."

"I think so, too," says Sasha. "But she was all sort of business-like and obviously flipping through a calendar, saying, 'Now let's see when can I fit you in,' and next Wednesday was evidently the first opening."

"Do you think she's planning to murder you?" Monique asks, finishing the last of her beer.

"No, because we're meeting at a bar on Amsterdam and Ninety-ninth," Sasha says. "It's not like she's luring me to some remote underpass."

"Not to change the subject," Monique says, digging into her

bag and pulling out a brochure. "But will you come with me to this singles volunteer thing tomorrow? We're refurbishing a brownstone for a needy family."

"I thought you were doing that singles grocery night thing," Sasha says. "On Thursdays."

"Well, I was until last Thursday!" Monique says, looking all het up. "When I had this long intense talk with a man in the checkout line and it turned out he works for Lambda Legal and was just there because he needed salad stuff."

"They should limit entrance to the store on those nights," Sasha says.

"So will you come with me?" Monique says. "Or, unless, I guess, now that Carson has left his wife, maybe you're not single anymore."

This sounds vaguely insulting, and more than a little negative, so Sasha says, "I'll see."

After meeting Monique, Sasha takes the subway down to Carson's club, where he's been staying for the past two weeks. Sasha loves his club—the threadbare stateliness of it, the way the staff flirt with her, the masculine rooms. She doesn't care if he lives there forever.

She happens to meet Carson in the lobby, where he is collecting his mail, and in the elevator, she tells him about the phone call.

He looks startled. "She called you?"

"Yes, and asked me out for a drink."

"Well, I don't think you should go," Carson says. "She's not a nice drunk."

The elevator stops and some other people get on, so Sasha is left to digest this piece of information in silence. Anne is not a nice drunk. She can add this to the only other two details Carson has ever revealed about Anne, which is that she works as an administrator for a nonprofit charity for the homeless and that it drives him crazy the way she never empties the fluff out of the dryer filter. Sasha wonders if it's some sort of flaw in her character that she was never more curious about Anne. Shouldn't she have been fascinated, eaten up by jealousy, followed them on marital outings?

Once they get to Carson's room, she says, "How is she not a nice drunk?"

Carson is flipping through his mail. "She just repeats herself endlessly. But she repeats herself endlessly when she's sober, too."

Another piece of information! Maybe Sasha should have been asking questions all along. "But why do you think she wants to meet me? Is she going to murder me?"

"Ha," says Carson, dumping his mail on the desk. "She might bore you to death, but otherwise you're pretty safe."

The fact that Carson finds Anne so boring is slightly shocking to Sasha. It seems to her that Carson is interested in everything. You could tell him a story without one single redeeming feature, like that the man at the bodega gave you Canadian money for change, and he would say, "Really? Which bodega was that?" (This actually happened to Sasha last week and she put the coins in her wallet and keeps accidentally trying to buy stuff with them and being yelled at by street vendors all over Manhattan.) The idea that Carson could be bored by anyone, let alone someone who maybe loves him, is distressing.

"And why did you tell her my name, anyway?" Sasha asks.

"She asked," Carson says. "The night I told her about the

affair. She said, 'Tell me about her, I want to know about this person who's so important to you.'"

Sasha says nothing. Carson told his wife about the affair two weeks ago. He said he hadn't meant to do it, but they were discussing their marriage and she was being all nice and sympathetic and told him he could tell her if there was someone else, that she would understand. Since then, he has said, somewhat cryptically, that her attitude seems to have "undergone a change." Even just thinking about this, it is hard for Sasha not to shake her head at the universal stupidity of men.

Sasha and Carson go out to dinner, just like a married couple. Well, maybe not a married couple, but a legitimate couple, at least, not caring anymore if anyone sees them. During dinner, he asks about the book Sasha is writing and Sasha is suddenly conscious of being boring. Should she be talking about Syria, or global warming?

It's only due to Carson that Sasha writes books at all. He was the one who encouraged her when an editor approached her about writing young adult romance novels, who told her, who cares if it's YA, you're still making a living by writing, and he was the one who sent her two dozen salmon-colored roses during the weekend in which she had to read two dozen young adult romances so that she could write the next one in the series. (She did it, too, though sometimes she feels she was never the same afterward.) And now Sasha, who never even had much of a job before, has a career, of sorts, and is offered four-book contracts and gets to stay home all day in her pajamas and really loves what she does. Also, Carson has proven exceptionally good at troubleshooting plot issues. The only person better at it is Monique, but she gets upset if Sasha doesn't use her ideas, and Carson doesn't seem to care. He can reel off a dozen possible solutions and doesn't mind if she rejects them all.

So she tells him that all the characters in this book live on an island and she needs to find a way for all of them to miss the last ferry home, and they discuss that for the rest of dinner.

Then they go back to Carson's room and get ready for bed, brushing their teeth together (another married couple thing!) and Carson spits in the sink and says, "I'm going to go apartment-hunting tomorrow, and I was hoping you'd come with me."

"I have to go to this volunteer thing with Monique," Sasha says, without planning to. "I already promised."

Sasha and Monique show up at the brownstone for the singles volunteer day, along with about thirty other people. The renovation is being run by a short and short-tempered redheaded man named Willie, who seems ready to shout at any of them with the slightest provocation. Sasha can understand why he's so grouchy, though: he has to oversee a bunch of volunteers who are all busy checking one another out instead of doing home repair. She almost feels a little sorry for the needy family who is going to move in, picturing the very low standard to which their new home will be refurbished.

Willie assigns them partners of the opposite sex and sets them to work on various tasks. Sasha's partner is a tall blond guy named Justin and their task is to remove the wallpaper in the living room. Every fifteen minutes, Willie blows a whistle and you can switch if you don't like your task (or, more likely, your partner, Sasha suspects).

Sasha and Justin mainly ignore each other and get on with their task. Even after the whistle blows four times, they're still working together. But when they finally take a break and go to the water cooler, Justin looks at her for a moment and Sasha suddenly knows, with an instinct born of long experience, that he is about to tell her that he has a girlfriend or to ask for her phone number. Or both.

And sure enough, Justin says in a low voice, "I have to tell you something. I'm not really single. I just came here because my friend Paul didn't want to come alone."

"Me, too," Sasha says. She hopes they are not going to have some long discussion about their respective relationships.

But Justin doesn't mention his girlfriend again. He only says, "I'm thinking maybe I should have a singles volunteer day at my apartment. It needs repainting and a whole bunch of other stuff."

"All my apartment really needs is a new door," Sasha says. "Or, actually, a new lock, because we left the coffeepot on a few weeks ago and the fire department had to break in and they damaged the lock and if we don't fix it eventually, the landlord will take it out of our security deposit."

"So you need to have a singles volunteer thing open only to locksmiths," Justin says.

"Well, everyone else could just hang out and have a few beers," Sasha says.

And then she is suddenly aware of trying to charm this man, and stops. Why should she charm him? She doesn't really like him. Who is he, anyway? He's not Carson.

When they say good-bye an hour later, Justin introduces his friend Paul to Monique, and maybe in an alternative universe, Paul and Monique would fall in love, but in actuality, Paul only smirks and says, "Yeah, I know you. You're the one who started painting before we'd primed the walls."

And Monique bristles and says, "Well, at least I didn't—"

But they are spared having to hear whatever she didn't do by the sound of something crashing upstairs, followed by a string of swearing from Willie.

Justin holds out his hand to Sasha. "Maybe I should give you my number in case you have that party," he says.

"It's for singles, remember," she says, but she shakes his hand.

She and Monique walk out into the baking August heat and Sasha thinks, as she always does when phone numbers are exchanged or nearly exchanged, about the time Monique shared a cab home from a party with a man and she wrote *I'd love to get together* on the back of one of her business cards and slid it in with her half of the cab fare and the man didn't call her but the cab driver did. It is among Sasha's fondest memories and she laughs out loud as they walk down the steps of the brownstone.

Sasha and Monique decide it is too hot to go back to their unair-conditioned apartment and so they go downtown and watch two movies in a row and eat a whole big box of popcorn and nearly an entire package of malted milk balls.

Then they walk very slowly uptown in the evening heat and go to the bar across the street from their apartment and start drinking Sea Breezes. After the first Sea Breeze, the man next to Sasha says that the man next to *him* is some sort of drunk migrant worker and buying everyone drinks. Sasha is fascinated: There are migrant workers in New York City? What exactly does he pick? But the migrant worker, if that's what he is, doesn't speak English and only gestures for Sasha and Monique to order more drinks, which they do and which he pays for, and Sasha feels a little bit bad about this but not that much.

After the fifth Sea Breeze (they are keeping track by folding the straws into triangles and poking them into the holes of the drainboard in the bar), a man smiles at Monique and she smiles back and then is swept with the horrifying realization that he's actually one of the guys who works at Broadway Bagel. So then Sasha and Monique have a long whispered discussion, wondering whether they are snobs for not wanting to socialize with him, and would they feel differently if he was, like, six inches taller, and since she smiled at him will Monique have to talk to him if he comes over, and does this mean they can't go to Broadway Bagel anymore? (The answer to all these questions, they decide, is probably.)

But after that, things pick up a bit, and they keep drinking and annoy the hell out of everyone by playing "Rescue Me" on the jukebox five times in a row. Then they walk home and Monique throws up in the lobby wastebasket and feels a little bit better, but Sasha doesn't and has to lie in the whirling pit of her bed with the box fan in the window set on high and blowing on her full blast, which is sort of like lying under the rotor of a Chinook helicopter while it tries to take off in a high altitude, but she's too drunk to get up and turn it down, and really, it's just a great day, a great evening. Perfect, in fact.

Oh, there is no limit to the things a real couple can do! They can call each other at any time of the day or night, without a lot of letting the phone ring and hanging up first. They can go out to brunch, which Sasha and Carson do on Sunday morning, as soon as her hangover recedes enough to allow movement. Somehow brunch was never a possibility when they were having an affair— the timing was all wrong. And Sasha doesn't have to debate end-lessly whether to wear her new white crocheted blouse because if Carson doesn't see it today, he'll see it tomorrow or the day after.

They can go to a bookstore together, they can wander up Lexington, they can go to Starbucks, they can go back to Carson's club for aspirin for Sasha's headache, they can go meet a friend of Carson's for drinks, and the drinks help Sasha's hangover even more than the aspirin. The friend they are meeting is a man from Carson's office, and he is nice enough, although when they are discussing the heat he says, "Imagine living through this without air-conditioning."

"My apartment doesn't have air-conditioning," Sasha says. "Actually, I've never lived in an apartment that does."

The man stares at her for a long moment, and Sasha wonders what he would say if she told him that in addition to not being air-conditioned, it's an unwritten rule in their building that all the neighbors take turns buying Budweiser for Mrs. Misner in 3C so she doesn't get all aggressive and shout things at their visitors.

Real couples don't have to decide whether to have sex or dinner, and after the sex and during the dinner, they can talk about going on vacation together, and Sasha can keep a nightgown and a toothbrush at Carson's club, whereas previously, anything of hers had to be small enough to fit in a locked drawer at his office. They can spend the night together, they can even spend two nights together. Time, which used to be their most precious commodity, they now have in abundance.

But they don't spend that second night together. When Carson asks why, Sasha is suddenly too shy to tell him that Monique has a first date with a guy she met at the singles volunteer day, and that Sasha would no more let Monique come home to an empty apartment after a first date than she would leave a small child outside crying in the cold. So she says she needs to look at a manuscript her editor sent and do her pages for the day, which is true, anyway.

So Sasha travels back uptown, sets up her laptop on the kitchen table, turns on the fans, makes herself some iced tea, and begins working.

She is still typing away when Monique bangs into the apartment, slams her bag on the table, and says, "If I were a cat, my ears would be straight back right now."

This tells Sasha everything she needs to know about the date, and also makes her laugh hard enough to spit iced tea all over the keyboard. She gets up for some paper towels and also to grab them each a beer out of the refrigerator, and she wishes, not for the first time, that life did not have to be a continuous series of eliminations, a constant narrowing of your options, a long series of choices in which you were always unhappy that you couldn't choose two things at the same time.

On Tuesday night, Sasha and Monique decide to go to the bar where Sasha is supposed to meet Anne and scope it out. It is a shockingly seedy place, even for this high up on Amsterdam Avenue, with decaying wood walls and a dank unpleasant smell.

"Oh, gross," says Monique as they walk in. "Why do you think she wants to meet *here*?"

"I don't know," says Sasha, but deep down she suspects she does know. Anne must think this bar is Sasha's counterpart, her equal in some way. She probably asked some of her homeless people where they go (or would go, since homeless people don't go out for drinks a lot).

"What can I get for you ladies?" the bartender says, startling Sasha because she hadn't actually seen him until that moment.

He is a tall, alarmingly thin man, and standing still in the dim light, he is nearly invisible.

They start toward the bar, but the bartender waves them off, saying, "Sit at the table! I'll bring your drinks over! What would you like?"

They both ask for Coronas and go sit at the table (there's only one), which has a scarred top; Monique's chair has one leg shorter than the others so she has to sit at a slight angle.

"Ew, he's putting the limes in our beers with his finger!" Monique whispers.

"Oh, it'll be fine," Sasha says. "The alcohol will kill the germs." (Won't it?)

The bartender walks over eagerly with their drinks. He seems to have a lot of energy for such a skinny, dried-out husk of a person. "There you go, pretty ladies," he says and then retreats back to the bar, where he watches them. He looks like an animated skeleton.

"So did Carson have any idea why Anne wants to meet you?" Monique asks.

Sasha shakes her head. "He knows nothing about it."

"Well, clearly she has some sort of agenda," Monique says, drinking her beer. "It's just that you don't know what it is. You're like Neville Chamberlain going to the Munich Conference."

"I guess," says Sasha, whose knowledge of world history is a little vague.

"Maybe she's going to ask you to give him back," Monique suggests. "Maybe she's going to say, 'I come to you in sisterhood and ask you to return him to me,' or something."

"Well, he's not really mine to return," Sasha says uncertainly. "And besides, he says that she doesn't act like she wants to get back together. He says she's very frosty."

"Oh, surprise!" Monique says. "He has a yearlong affair with a twenty-six-year-old blonde and his wife is frosty about it!"

Sasha blinks. She wishes she could shake the feeling sometimes that Monique sympathizes with Anne entirely too much.

"So, can I ask why *you're* going?" Monique says. "Why didn't you just tell her it wasn't a good idea? You could still call and cancel."

"I don't know why I agreed," Sasha says, and at the time of the original phone call it was true. But now she supposes she agreed to go because it was interesting. Life is full of good things—buttered toast, cold beer, compelling books, campfires, Christmas lights, expensive lipstick, the smell of vanilla—and Sasha is by no means immune to them, but how many things are just flat-out *interesting*? How many things are so fascinating that you can't stand not to do them? Not many, is Sasha's opinion.

"Well, what are you going to wear?" Monique asks. "I think you should wear your green blouse and your black pencil skirt."

Sasha knows that this is what Monique would wear. They are the same height and weight and even have the same hair color, but everything about Monique is sharp angles, including her hair, which is cut in a perfect slant toward her chin. Sasha's hair is long and unruly and she wears jeans and T-shirts almost all the time. And sometimes when she is finishing writing a book, she wears the *same* jeans and T-shirt for days on end, for good luck.

"And definitely your Egyptian earrings," Monique says.

Sasha smiles. "Okay, definitely those."

The bartender, who by now is really giving Sasha the creeps, does his springy walk again and brings them two more beers. "These are on the house," he says.

So they drink the beers and Monique notices a sign above the bar for cream of potato soup and says she'd rather shoot herself than eat anything served here, and Sasha says it's so disturbing that the word *potato* is in quotes, like maybe it's not made from real potatoes, and Monique says it almost certainly isn't, and they discuss the new tailor shop that opened near them and put up a sign saying FOR ALL YOUR TAILORING "NEEDS" and what are *those* quotes supposed to signify? And they talk for a while about when they moved into their current apartment and one of the movers turned out to be a guy that Sasha had started to give her number to at a bar but at the last minute changed her mind and gave him just a bunch of random digits and how that made moving day so much more hellish than it already was. This actually happened three years ago, but they still discuss it fairly frequently.

Sasha does not know what this kind of conversation is called. It is not small talk, and it is not gossip precisely, nor is it deep and meaningful discussion. *Dialogue, meeting, palaver, visit*—none of them seem quite right. If there is a term, Sasha is unaware of it. She only knows she never wants to be without it in her life. Never, never, never.

Sasha is twenty minutes late to her meeting with Anne, because she tends to be ten minutes late wherever she goes and also because she spent an extra ten minutes looking for her Egyptian earrings.

So she has to hurry into the bar, feeling sweaty and rumpled, and right away she regrets her visit here last night with Monique because the cadaverous bartender says, "Well, hello, again!" making her sound like a regular.

Anne is sitting at the lone table (is in fact the only person in the bar) and though Sasha supposes it could be some random woman and not Anne, she's very sure it is.

She hurries over and pulls out the chair opposite Anne. "Sorry I'm late," she says. "I lost track of time."

Anne is regarding her coolly. Maybe she doesn't like the idea of Sasha losing track of time before their big meeting. Finally she says, "You're younger than I thought but not as pretty."

Sasha wipes a little moisture from her upper lip. "Well, all my life I've wanted to be this cool elegant beauty," she says, "and in reality I think I'm more a friendly blonde a lot of men have wanted to have sex with. Though that was pretty nice, too."

If Anne looks shocked by this, it's no more than Sasha is. (Imagine Neville Chamberlain saying such a thing!) She resolves to think before she speaks again. Although she has no intention of saying so, she thinks that actually the reverse is true of Anne— she is older but prettier than Sasha had imagined. Anne has very pale skin, though to Sasha it looks strangely devoid of pores, and black hair cut in a short bob. Her eyes are pale blue with dark lashes. It's a Snow White kind of pretty and completely the opposite of Sasha, who has quite a few freckles. Also, Anne is wearing a dark blue suit, with an expensive-looking patterned silk scarf tied around her throat. Sasha can never wear scarves. She always takes them off and stuffs them in her purse after half an hour.

There is a long beat of silence and then Anne says, "Perhaps we should get a bottle of wine."

"I don't think they sell it by the bottle here," Sasha says. "Only by the glass."

"Two glasses of wine, then," Anne says.

They both look at the bartender but he is sitting behind the bar, avoiding eye contact, and showing no signs of coming over to them. Evidently that's something he does only on rare occasions, or for two girls in their twenties.

"I'll have red wine," Anne says, as though Sasha is the waitress. Sasha feels a sudden flash of compassion for Carson. Is this what their life together was like?

But she doesn't really see a point in arguing, so she crosses the bar and orders two glasses of house red from the bartender, who becomes spookily animated again and says, "With pleasure, my lovely!" and Sasha is really starting to wish they'd gone somewhere, anywhere, else.

When she returns to the table with the glasses of wine, Anne says, "I hear you used to be a receptionist and now you're a writer." She says this the way someone might say, *I hear you used to be a junkie and now you're a prostitute.*

Sasha has a sudden bad-tempered urge to tell Anne how supportive Carson is of her writing, how if she hasn't finished her pages for the day, he'll sit in her living room, reading fashion magazines or watching *Unsolved Mysteries* with Monique, even on nights when they have only an hour or two to spend together.

Perhaps Anne senses her misstep because she says, "I hear you write children's books," in a slightly friendlier tone.

Are they not supposed to mention Carson's name? Why does Anne keep saying *I hear* as though she and Sasha have some large circle of mutual friends?

"Well, young adult books," Sasha says. "More for teenagers." Perhaps Anne thought she illustrated children's books and was picturing some large friendly girl who dressed like Raggedy Ann and had a sunny outlook.

Then they enter into quite an extraordinary period of conversation, lasting through this glass of wine and the next one (which Sasha also has to go get), during which they discuss publishing, romance writing, and whether or not anyone actually reads poetry anymore. Sasha, who is drinking her wine in big nervous gulps, wonders if she should tell Anne about the time she got very drunk at a publishing party and explained to a famous poet what slant rhyme is. (This is an extremely funny story, but not everyone seems to appreciate it.)

And it is at precisely this point that Anne leans forward slightly and says, "You know, Carson won't stay with you."

Sasha blinks. She had almost forgotten who Anne was.

Anne smiles grimly. "He's just cunt struck, is all."

The writer in Sasha rushes forward to examine this sentence. *Cunt struck.* The term is so ugly, yet so arresting, that she almost admires it. Maybe she could use it in a book someday. But the rest of Sasha is cringing. *Cunt struck* hangs before her like it's written in an angry black scrawl. Does Anne really think it applies to her, to Carson and her?

"You think you can just take whatever you want, whether it belongs to you or not," Anne says, and now her voice is shaking. "You're a home-wrecker, and you have no morals at all."

Two things occur to Sasha at this instant. One: Having morals is not something she's ever aspired to. Successful writer, loyal friend, pretty girl; those have been goals, but she can't say *moral person* has ever made the list, and that's kind of startling to realize. Two (and this possibly should have occurred to her quite a while ago): She doesn't have to sit here and listen to this. She can leave.

So she does. She pushes back her chair and walks right out of the bar. Does it worry her that she's left Anne to settle the bill? No. Does it bother her that Anne may be molested or harassed by the world's scariest bartender? Not at all. Is she even a little concerned that Anne may come out of the bar and not have enough sense to walk toward Broadway instead of Columbus and be murdered for the money in her pocketbook and her pricey scarf? Not one bit. In fact, Sasha feels like right now she herself could walk toward Columbus with impunity. She has no morals, right? The muggers and murderers would see her as one of their own, and stay out of her way.

Sasha walks almost twenty blocks downtown in a sort of daze before she thinks to use her cell phone. She paws through her bag and is relieved to find her phone (suppose she had to go back for it!). Maybe she should be calling Carson right now, but that's not who she wants to speak to. She calls Monique at work.

"It's—me," Sasha says, and her voice breaks so harshly between the two words that it sounds like a badly spliced tape.

"Oh, my God!" Monique says. "How was it? Are you okay? Is she holding you at gunpoint? If you need me to call the police, just say the word *leopard* in your next sentence."

Sasha leans against the side of a building. She feels as though the world has come back into focus. "I don't need you to call the police," she says. "And if I did, how I am supposed to work the word *leopard* in unobtrusively?"

"Well, I don't know," Monique says. "I was trying to pick a word you wouldn't say accidentally, like *street* or *bagel*. And you just did say leopard."

"Yes, but I don't need you to call the police," Sasha says. "I just need you to meet me somewhere."

"Okay, all right, just a minute," Monique says, apparently thinking out loud. "I'll tell them I'm working from home— hardly anybody's here anyway. Are you on Broadway? I'll start walking up."

Sasha *is* on Broadway so she keeps walking downtown. She does not want to think about Anne, so she thinks about Monique and the code word *leopard* some more. They will have to come up with a foolproof one. Monique is right, it should be something that they wouldn't say accidentally. She wonders what the top ten words they use are, anyway. Let's think: *street, bagel, bar, guy, book, sleep, write, rent, shower, beer* are probably all up there. So possibly *leopard* was a good choice, or maybe *zygote* or *plankton*. Sasha and Monique also have a contingency plan in case one of them is ever wanted by the police and has to go on the run. They will meet the first Monday of every month in the Au Bon Pain in Times Square, and exchange money or messages or whatever is needed. They once spent a long and very pleasurable evening working this out, and what Sasha thinks most people don't realize is that they would actually do this for each other, indefinitely, no question about it.

Sasha looks up and sees Monique down the block, and has that thrill you get from seeing someone familiar on the streets of New York, like looking through a box of old paperbacks at a garage sale and finding a copy of a novel you love. And this time the pleasure is intensified because Sasha is not just running into some random acquaintance. Monique is hurrying straight toward her, a look of concern on her face. Her roommate, who has left work early, and who would have called the police if need be.

She doesn't need to wonder anymore. Monique is on Sasha's side, that's whose.

Now here is something interesting: Sasha doesn't tell Monique about the term *cunt struck* but it never occurs to her not to tell Carson. It is the kind of detail that Monique would remember, though she might never bring it up again, where it seems like Carson ignores everything about Sasha that doesn't fit with his perception of her. She can tell him anything.

She is in Carson's room at his club, sitting in front of the air conditioner in her nightgown, drinking a very small bottle of whiskey from the minibar, while Carson rubs her feet. She went out for Indian food with Monique and had several more glasses of red wine.

"First, she said I was younger than she thought I'd be but not as pretty," Sasha says, loudly, because of the air conditioner.

Carson laughs. "Well, you don't know whether that's a compliment or an insult," he says, "because you don't know the known parameters."

But Sasha doesn't want to get drawn into a mathematical discussion. She tells him the rest of it, and when she gets to the *cunt struck* part, it doesn't seem so awful to her anymore, not really, but Carson squeezes her foot tightly, almost painfully. She looks at his face and his expression is harder, stonier, than she has ever seen it before. She realizes suddenly that although Carson has said from the beginning that his wife didn't understand him (you cannot imagine Monique's scorn at this phrase) it is actually true. Anne does not understand him, or does not understand him well enough, to know that saying what she did would make Carson angry. But Sasha knew, she realizes. That's why she told him.

Sasha shakes her foot gently so he will release it, which he does and reaches for his own drink.

"Monique said Anne had an agenda," she says. "And evidently it was to tell me what an awful person I am."

Carson smiles. Whatever he feels about what Anne said, he's apparently going to keep to himself. "I like the way you not only tell me what happened to you, you tell me what Monique thinks about it."

Interestingly, Monique feels almost the opposite about this, and never wants to hear what Carson thinks about anything. Sasha wonders if this makes Carson a nicer person than Monique. Monique would argue that no, someone who cheats on his wife is by definition not a nice person. How would the four of them—Sasha, Monique, Anne, Carson—rank from nicest to least nice? A sudden alcohol-induced yawn makes her jaws ache and Sasha finds she is too tired to worry about it. She gets out of her chair and crawls into the bed.

"Where did you meet her, anyway?" Carson asks, beginning to get undressed.

"Some bar on Amsterdam," Sasha says, yawning again. "If it had a name, I don't remember it."

"I saw an apartment today that I liked," Carson says. "I have an appointment to see it again on Friday. Will you come look at it?"

Sasha nods, but is not paying attention. She thinks of all the bars and restaurants along Broadway between 106th and Thirty-sixth and how she and Monique have met for dinner or drinks in almost all of them (this could be the reason they never seem to have any money) and she realizes that Anne could have picked one of those places and then Sasha would have felt bad every time she walked past it, and it would have ruined whatever happy memory she had of being there. But instead Anne chose a bar Sasha had never been to, where she wasn't known, which she didn't even like. Sasha never has to go there again.

· ·

Sasha probably would have slept right through the appointment with the real estate agent on Friday except that Monique called and woke her to say that she'd just talked to the Brooklyn branch of her office. When they were all on the Upper West Side two weeks ago and went drinking and then had slices of Koronet Pizza with her and Sasha, they all got severe food poisoning, with two of them ending up in the hospital.

"But it can't have been from the pizza," Sasha says, "because we all bought slices, and you and I didn't get sick."

"Exactly!" Monique says. "Apparently we're immune because we eat there so much."

"I don't know whether to be excited or worried," Sasha says.

"Excited," Monique says definitively. "We're like some new super-species!"

After that it's impossible to go back to sleep, so Sasha gets up and gets dressed and goes to meet Carson and the real estate agent. She's only fifteen minutes late, which is really only five minutes late for her, but she can see as she approaches that the agent is tense, though Carson looks relaxed.

"Hello," Sasha says, as she walks up to the building's entrance, where they are waiting for her.

"You must be Sasha," the real estate agent says. She's a woman in her thirties with spiky brown hair and Sasha can tell from her expression that she was expecting Sasha to be different some-how, more sophisticated, maybe. She wonders if that's going to be her life from now on if she stays with Carson, people expecting her to be something she's not.

The apartment is on the third floor of a building on East Sixty-seventh Street, directly across from an ice cream store called Peppermint Park. These are both strikes against it because

Sasha has always felt she doesn't belong on the Upper East Side, and besides, how much weight would she gain with an ice cream parlor right across the street?

But she and Carson and the real estate agent go up and tour the apartment, and Sasha decides that the main thing wrong with it is that there's nothing wrong with it. She and Monique concluded long ago that you're not really living in New York unless there's something wildly negative about your apartment, like the one they lived in where the shower was in the kitchen, or the one in the building *The New York Times* dubbed "the house of horrors" because so many people committed suicide there. In their current apartment, you can roll a marble downhill from the front door to the back of the kitchen.

The real estate agent says, "I know Carson especially liked this place because it has a room for you to write in. It's just a little hidey-hole, but I think you'll like it."

The real estate agent leads her to an extremely small sunny room with a perfectly square window, and just enough space for a desk and a writer. Currently, Sasha has no desk, she has to use the kitchen table after she clears Monique's breakfast dishes off it, and the only view is across the air shaft into their neighbor's kitchen. This has never bothered Sasha, though. She does not even know where she is ten minutes after she starts typing.

She walks over and looks out the window of the hidey-hole, wishing that the stupid real estate agent had not called it that because now she doubts she can ever think of it any other way.

Carson comes up behind her and puts his arms around her. "Do you like this room?"

"I love it," Sasha says. But really, she is thinking that Monique would love it. She would love that Carson chose an apartment with a room for Sasha to write in. Finally, he has done something Monique would approve of and this thought gives Sasha a little stab of sorrow, as sharp as a splinter.

Carson rests his chin on the top of her head and Sasha leans back against him. Across the street, a man and four children have come out of Peppermint Park, and the man is holding four cones and some napkins, while the children jump up and down around him like pigeons around a picnicker.

"They look happy, don't they?" Carson asks.

"Yes," Sasha says softly, but she is wondering how anyone else can think they are happy at this particular moment, when she alone knows the meaning of happiness. She holds it right now in the palm of her hand.

HOW TO GIVE THE WRONG IMPRESSION

You never refer to Boris as your roommate, although of course that's exactly what he is. You're actually apartment mates and you only moved in together the way any two friends move in together for the school year, nothing romantic. Probably Boris would be horrified if he knew how you felt. You're a psych major, you know this is unhealthy, but when you speak of him you always say Boris, or, better yet, *This guy I live with*. He may be just your roommate but not everyone has to know.

You buy change-of-address cards with a picture on the front, of a bear packing a trunk. You send them to your friends and your parents. After some hesitation, you write "Boris and Gwen" on the back, above the address. After all, he does live here.

You help Boris buy a bed. This is a great activity for you, it's almost like being engaged. You lie on display beds with him in furniture stores. Toward the end of the day, you are tired and spend longer and longer just resting on the beds.

Boris lies next to you, telling you about the time his sister peed in a display toilet at Sears when she was three. You glance at him sideways. He looks tired, too, although the whites of his eyes are still bright—the kind of eyes you thought only blue-eyed people had, but his eyes are brown.

A salesman approaches, sees you, smiles. He knocks on the frame of the bed with his knuckles. "Well, what do you folks think?" he asks.

Boris turns to you. You ask the salesman about interest rates, delivery fees, assembly charges. You never say, *Well, it's your bed, Boris,* in front of the salesman.

When your parents come through town and offer to take you and Boris out to dinner, you accept. But this is risky, this all depends on whether you've implied anything to your parents beyond what was on the change-of-address card. You think about it and decide it's pretty safe, but you spend a great deal of time hoping your father will not ask Boris what his intentions are.

Boris, love of your life, goes to the salad bar three times and doesn't stick a black olive on each of his fingers, a thing he often does at home. On the way out, he holds your hand. You are the picture of young love. Boris may make the folks' annual Christmas letter.

You always have boyfriends. You try to get them taller than Boris, but it's not easy. Sometimes after they pick you up, they roll their shoulders uncomfortably in the elevator and say, "Gwen, I think Boris is going to slash my tires or something, he's so jealous."

Snort. "Oh, please," you say. Later, during a lull in the conversation, you ask casually, "What makes you think Boris is jealous of you?" One of your boyfriends says it's because Boris found six hundred excuses to come into the living room while you two were drinking wine. Another one says it's the way Boris shook hands with him. This is interesting. You were still in your bedroom when that happened.

Whatever they answer, you file it away and replay it later in your mind.

You always encourage Boris to ask Dahlia Kosinski out.

When he comes back from his ethics study group and says, "Oh, my God, Dahlia looked so incredibly gorgeous tonight," you do not say, *I heard she almost got kicked out of the ethics class for sleeping with the professor.* You say, "I think you should ask her out."

"Noooo," Boris says, drawing circles on the kitchen table with his pencil.

"Sure," you say. "Just pick up the phone." In fact, you do pick up the phone. You call information and get Dahlia's number. Say, "Want me to dial?"

Boris shakes his head. "Let's go get something to eat," he says. He puts his arms around you and dances you away from the phone. You think that Dahlia Kosinski is probably too tall for Boris's chin to rest on her head like this.

You didn't write Dahlia's phone number down on the scratch pad by the phone when you called information, because you don't need Boris looking at it and mulling it over when you're not around. This whole procedure is nerve-racking, but not to worry—he'll never ask her out, and it's always, always better to know than to wonder.

In Pigeon Lab, you name your pigeon after him because the two other women who work there name their pigeons after their husbands. You spend a lot of time making fun of Boris when these two women make fun of their husbands. This, as a matter of fact, is not hard to do.

You tell them about how he keeps a flare gun in the trunk of his car. Ask them how many times they think his car is going to break down in the middle of the Mojave Desert or at sea.

You tell them that he has this thing for notebooks. He keeps one in the glove compartment of his car and records all this information in it whenever he fills the gas tank. You say, "I mean, there can be four hundred cars behind us at the gas station, honking, and there's Boris, frantically scribbling down the number of gallons and the price and everything."

They are so amused by this that you tell them he has another notebook where he records all the cash he spends. You say, "If he leaves a waitress two dollars, he runs home and writes it down." You add, "I'm surprised he doesn't also record the serial numbers."

Because this last part isn't even about Boris, it's about your father, you worry that you are becoming a pathological liar.

You never act jealous in front of Linette, his best friend from undergrad. She spends the day at your apartment on her way to a game she's going to be in. She plays basketball for some college in California.

She is as tall and slender as you feared and not as coarse and brawny as you wanted. You had hoped she would lope around the apartment, pick you up, and chuck you to Boris, saying, *Well, Bo, I guess we could toss a little thing like her right through the hoop.*

Actually, Boris and Linette do go play some basketball, and when they come back, you all sit on the couch and drink beer. Linette puts her hand on Boris's thigh, which is lightly sweating, and you hope it's just from basketball. You resist the urge to put your hand on his other thigh. You imagine yourself and Linette frantically claiming Boris's body parts, slapping your hands on his legs, then his arms, then his chest. Only knowing how much pleasure he would get out of this keeps you from doing it.

Instead, you finish your beer in one long swig, anxious to show that you can drink right along with any basketball player, and you rise. You say, "It's been nice to meet you, Linette, but I have to go, I have a date." You don't have boyfriends anymore, just dates.

"Yes," you say again, "I have to go get ready." You say this so Linette will believe that you are looking the way you normally look around the house, that you are actually about to go make yourself better-looking. She does not need to know that you're already wearing a lot of makeup, that this is about as good as it gets.

You pretend you don't want to kiss him. He calls from a bar on Halloween, too drunk to drive, when you are home studying. You drive to pick him up, wearing sweats and your glasses. You wear your glasses only on nights when you don't plan to see him.

He sings on the ride home, pulling on your braid. Wonder why he's in such a good mood. Was Dahlia Kosinski at this bar?

In the kitchen, he drinks your orange juice out of the carton. You say, "Put that back."

Boris says, "Too late," and holds the carton upside down to demonstrate. Three drops of orangey water fall on the floor.

"Damn," you say and throw the sponge on the floor. This is a good indication of how irritable you are, because the floor was already sticky enough to rip your socks off.

"I'm sorry, Gwen," Boris says. "I'll go get more tomorrow, I promise."

"Forget it," you say, rubbing the sponge around with your toe.

"If you forgive me, I'll kiss you," Boris says.

Now you don't even have to pretend you don't want to kiss him, because, you have to face it, that was pretty obnoxious.

"Oh, spare me," you say, and cross your arms over your chest. Boris leans over and kisses you on the eyebrow. Don't in any way change your posture, but you can close your eyes.

He touches your lips with his tongue. Wonder why you have to suffer this mutant behavior on top of everything else. He must look like someone trying to be the Human Mosquito. Does this even count as a kiss? This is a very good question, and you will spend no small amount of time pondering it.

Boris cuts himself shaving and leaves big drops of blood on the sink. You approach cautiously; it looks as if a small animal had been murdered.

You consider your options. You could point silently but dramatically at the sink when Boris returns. You could leave him an amused but firm note: "Dear Boris, I don't even want to know what happened in here. . . ." Or you can do nothing and assume that he'll eventually do something about it. That is probably your best option. But what if he thinks you left it there? What if he thinks you shave your legs in the sink or something? Best to clean it up and not mention it.

This you do, pushing a paper towel around the sink with a spoon.

· ·

You take Boris home for Thanksgiving dinner. All goes smoothly except for your grandmother glaring at him after the turkey is carved and announcing, "The one thing I will not tolerate is this living together, and I say that aloud for all the young people to hear."

Boris looks up from his turkey drumstick like a startled wolf cub, a spot of grease smeared on his cheek.

Later, when you are walking back toward the train station, he says, "What did your grandmother mean by that?"

Hoot. You say, "I don't know, but the way she said 'all the young people' made it sound like there were a whole group of young people, drinking beer or something."

Boris is not to be distracted. "The thing is," he says, "we aren't living together in *that* way."

You try not to wince. You do shiver. You take Boris's hand as he bounds along on his long legs, your signal that he has to either slow down or pull you along. He tucks both your hand and his hand into the pocket of his jacket. You look up at his face out of the corner of your eye. In the cold, you watch him breathe perfect plumes of white that match the sheepskin lining of his jacket. You think how happy you would be if Boris thought you were half as beautiful as you think he is at this moment.

You walk this way for a few minutes. Then he tells you that your hand is sweating, making a lake in his pocket, and gives you his gloves to wear.

You take to going out with Boris for frozen yogurt almost every night at about midnight. You are always the last people in the yogurt place, and the guy who works there closes up around you. Tonight Boris says, "Gwen, you have hot fudge in the corner of your mouth," and wipes it away, hard, with the ball of his thumb. Wonder if you feel too comfortable with him to truly be in love.

But then he licks the fudge off his thumb and smiles at you, his hair still ruffled from the wind outside. He is the love of your life, no question about it.

For Christmas, you buy Boris a key chain. This is what you had always imagined you would give a boyfriend someday, a key chain with a key to your apartment. Only it's not exactly a parallel situation with Boris, of course, in that he's not your boyfriend and he already has a key to your apartment, because he lives there. Okay, you admit it, there are no parallels other than that you are giving him a key chain.

Still, you can tell the guy in the jewelry store anything you like. Go ahead, say it: "This is for my boyfriend, do you think he'll like it?"

For Christmas, Boris gives you a framed poster of the four major food groups. You amuse yourself by trying to think of one single more unromantic gift he could have given you. You amuse yourself by wondering if you can make this into an anecdote for the women in Pigeon Lab.

When people ask you what Boris gave you for Christmas, you smile shyly and insinuate that you were both too broke to afford much.

The girls in Pigeon Lab have a Valentine's Day party and invite you and Boris. Probably you shouldn't show him the invitation, since his name is on it and he might wonder why you and he are invited as a couple. Just say, "Look, I have a party to go to, want to come?"

"Sure," Boris says, and the best part of the whole thing is that this way you know without asking that he doesn't have plans with someone else.

You don't have boyfriends anymore, and these days you don't even have dates. You tell Boris this is because you have too much work to do, and often on Saturday nights you make a big production of hauling your *Psychology of Women* textbook out to the sofa and propping it on your lap, even though it hurts your thighs and you never read it.

Instead, you talk to Boris, who is similarly positioned on the other end of the sofa, his feet touching yours. Sometimes he lies with his head in your lap and falls asleep that way. You never get up and leave him; you stay, touching his hair, idly clicking through the channels, watching late-night rodeo.

One night Boris wakes up during the calf roping. "Oh, my God," he says, watching a calf do a four-legged split, its heavy head wobbling. "This is breaking my heart."

This thing with Dahlia Kosinski reminds you of a book you read as a child, *Good News, Bad News*.

The good news is the ethics study group has a party and Boris invites you to go. The bad news is that Dahlia Kosinski is there and she's beautiful in a careless, sloppy way you know you never will be: shaggy black hair, too much black eyeliner, a leopard-print dress with a stain on the shoulder. You know that her nylons have a big run somewhere and she doesn't even care. The good news is that Dahlia has heard of you. "Hello," she says. "Are you Gwen?" The bad news is that she makes some joke about a book she read once called *Gwendolyn the Miracle Hen,* and Boris laughs. The good news is that Dahlia has what appears to be a very serious boyfriend. The bad news is that they have a fight in the bathroom, so maybe they're not really in love. The worse news is that in the car on the way home Boris says, "I don't think Dahlia will ever leave that boyfriend of hers. Everyone I've talked to says they're very serious." Which means that he's looked into Dahlia's love life, he's made inquiries. Wonder how there can be bad news followed by worse news. Does that ever happen in the book? Bad news: You're pushed out of an airplane. Worse news: You don't have a parachute?

Boris tells you that one night he stopped by the frozen yogurt place without you and the guy behind the counter made some sort of pass at him and wanted to know if you were Boris's girlfriend.

Ask, "What did you tell him?"

"What choice did I have?" Boris says in a tone that crushes you like a grape.

Linette stops by again. This time she spends the night, disappearing into Boris's room with a six-pack. You hear them laughing in there. Whatever else you do, call someone and go out that night.

When you are in the kitchen the next morning, Boris wanders out. You ask him how he feels. "Tired," he says. "Linette kept me up all night talking about whether she should go to grad school or not."

Wonder if he's telling the truth. Say, "Should she?"

"God, no," Boris says. "She's such a birdbrain."

"Oh," you say loudly, over the banging of your heart.

You clean the bathroom late one night after Boris has gone to bed. You wear a T-shirt and a pair of Boris's boxer shorts that you stole out of a bag of stuff he's been planning to take to the Salvation Army. It gives you immense pleasure to wear these boxer shorts, but you wear them only after he's gone to bed, and you never sleep in them. You do have some pride.

Your cleaning is ambitious: you wipe the tops of the doors, the inside of the shower curtain; you even unscrew the drain and pull out a hair ball the size of a rat terrier. It is so amazing that you consider taking a picture with your smiling face next to it for size reference, but in the end you just throw it out.

You are standing on the edge of the tub, balancing a bowl of hot, soapy water on your hip and swiping at the shower-curtain rod with a sponge when Boris walks in and says, "Well, hello, Mrs. Clean."

You smile. He yawns. "Do you need some help?" he says.

You let him hold the bowl of water while you turn your back to him and reach up and run the sponge along the shower-curtain rod.

"I never knew you had to clean those," Boris says. "I can't believe it's one in the morning. I feel like we're married and this is our first apartment or something."

Your throat closes. Until this moment you had not thought about the fact that this was your and Boris's first apartment, that once the lease is up there might not be a second apartment, and you might not see him every day.

"Hey," says Boris. "You're wearing my boxer shorts." He puts the bowl of water on the sink and turns the waistband inside out so he can read the tag. "They are!" he says, delighted.

You freeze. Clear your throat. "Yeah, well," you say.

Even standing on the edge of the tub, you are only a few inches taller than Boris, and he slides an arm around your waist. He brushes your hair forward over your shoulders and traces a *V* on your back for a long moment, as though you were a mannequin and he were a fashion designer contemplating some new creation.

Then you feel him kiss the back of your neck above your T-shirt. You remember Halloween and think about saying, *Boris, are those your lips?* but you don't. You don't do anything. You still haven't moved; your arms are over your head, hands braced against the rod.

"You're so funny, Gwen," Boris whispers against your skin.

"Really?" you say. A drop of soapy water lands on your eyelid, soft as cotton, warm as wax. "Me?"

SINGLE, CAREFREE, MELLOW

....

You could sum it up this way: Maya's dog was dying, and she was planning to leave her boyfriend of five years. On the whole, she felt worse about the dog.

"God, that's horrible," said Rhodes, Maya's boyfriend. "I don't know if I can stand it. There's really nothing we can do?"

He was talking about the dog dying, because he didn't know that part about Maya leaving him yet. Though if he had, he might well have said exactly the same thing. And then Maya would have had to say, *No, there's nothing we can do. It's like that song: You just can't be here, now that my heart is gone.*

Yesterday morning, Maya's dog, Bailey, a yellow Labrador, had refused to eat breakfast. This behavior was so extremely out of character (Maya could in fact never remember it having happened before) that both Maya and Rhodes were immediately concerned. Maya made some scrambled eggs for Bailey, and while she was doing that, Rhodes examined Bailey and discovered a marble-size lump in her cheek.

Maya had felt a hot ember of resentment about the fact that Rhodes had found this lump before she did. Bailey was *her* dog, had been her dog since she was eighteen, had been her dog for exactly twice as long as Rhodes had been her boyfriend. Maya should have been checking for the lump instead of scrambling eggs as a displacement activity. She felt marginally vindicated when Bailey ate the eggs, though, and then she drove Bailey straight over to the veterinary clinic.

The vet had done a biopsy and had called to tell Maya that Bailey had an extremely aggressive form of cancer, and would most likely not live more than six or eight weeks.

Maya hung up with the vet and immediately called Rhodes. Because the problem was, of course, that although sometimes Maya's heart was gone, sometimes it came back. Sometimes she could actually feel it thump back into her chest so hard it made her rib cage rattle. And then she would have to see Rhodes, would have to put her arms around his thin body and kiss him, even though he was too tall to kiss comfortably, would have to touch his face and brush his hair out of his eyes, and hear his voice, even if he was saying something unbearably boring about computers to somebody else, like, "NFS keeps timing out and locking up my whole system."

There were times when nothing but Rhodes would do.

That night, Maya and Rhodes had dinner at Rhodes's parents' house, which was just across town. They did this about once a week and Maya had always been grateful that she and Rhodes were not required to give up their weekends, just one week-night. Rhodes's family was accepting and relaxed, and for the most part, it was easy to be around them. As opposed to her own family, who lived across the country and when they were there for Christmas last year, Rhodes had hugged her mother and her mother had asked if he was drunk (which he had been, incredibly so, but that was not the point).

But today Rhodes's mother, Hazelene, rushed up to Maya and embraced her so fiercely that Maya wondered if there had been a terrorist attack or natural disaster in the fifteen minutes it had taken her and Rhodes to drive over.

"My dear," Hazelene said. "You must be devastated. Rhodes called me in tears as soon as you got the news about Bailey."

"Oh," said Maya, understanding. "Yes, well, it's horrible."

She was a little shocked to learn that Rhodes had called his mother, called her *in tears* apparently. She tried to think if she would have done this if things were reversed. Rhodes did not have any pets but he did have a lumpen sixteen-year-old sister named Magellan (they all had idiotic names, the whole family; there was a brother named Pegasus). Would Maya have called her own mother in tears if Magellan were given six weeks to live? In all honestly, she wasn't sure she would have. But then Bailey lived with them (Magellan, thank God, did not) and Bailey loved Rhodes with a devotion, which, in a human, would border on the insane. Whereas Magellan, apart from a brief period of infatuation two years ago when she painted Maya's fingernails dark blue, did not seem to like Maya all that much.

Like later, during dinner when Rhodes's father, Desmond, said, "Can someone explain to me who the Jonas Brothers are and why they wear chastity belts?" and Maya attempted to catch Magellan's eye to exchange a look of commiseration and Magellan said, "Why are you staring at me? Do you want me to pass the butter?"

What could you do with a person like that? Maya was an only child and she had always hoped she would be close to her boyfriend's sisters, that they would become like her own sisters. And right at that moment, during dinner, she realized that this still might happen. Not with Magellan (obviously) but with some other boyfriend's sister, the boyfriend after Rhodes. The idea of this filled Maya with a feeling so sparkly, so effervescent, that she could only gaze around the table, wondering why everyone did not sense this about her, why they could not see she was poised for flight.

Maya worked two days a week as a collection management librarian at the university, and the other three days a week, she worked from home as a website designer, mostly for schools and libraries. The director of the library was a man named Gildas-Joseph, who had a very faint French accent and the first glints of silver showing in the hair by his temples. Maya found him wildly attractive, although she knew that if she were actually single and started dating him, she would quickly find something about him highly annoying, most likely the fact of his wife and children.

Maya told Gildas-Joseph that she had to leave early, for personal reasons, and didn't add that the personal reason was taking Bailey to the vet.

Gildas-Joseph just looked at her with his dark eyes, and said, "Of course, Maya," and Maya thought again how sexy he was.

She took Bailey to the clinic, and this time they saw a different vet, Dr. Drummond. He was tall, with a short, almost military haircut, and very light blue eyes. Maya found *him* attractive, too. This was part of why she felt she should leave Rhodes, this business of finding all sorts of other men attractive.

Dr. Drummond sat on the floor, petting Bailey and stroking

the unswollen side of her face while Maya said, "She's not eating very much, and when she does, sometimes her mouth bleeds a little. Also that thing on her cheek looks bigger to me."

Dr. Drummond gently pried Bailey's mouth open and shone a light inside. "The tumor is invading her mouth," he said. He paused. "I think we may be talking about two weeks or so now."

Maya did not think she would cry but when she tried to talk, her voice was all wobbly. "Two weeks? That's all?"

Dr. Drummond nodded. "I can give her a shot, a painkiller, but I'd like to see her again in a few days."

Maya said nothing. Dr. Drummond gave Bailey the shot, which made her whimper, and then he broke a dog biscuit into tiny bits and fed them to her slowly.

Then he glanced at Maya's face. "Let me walk you to your car," he said.

Maya went to the receptionist, but was just waved away (evidently when your dog was dying, they billed you later) and she and Dr. Drummond and Bailey walked out to the car. Dr. Drummond helped Bailey climb in and then he stood next to Maya.

"Are you okay to drive?" he asked.

She nodded, and he held her hand. There in the parking lot, he held her hand.

In just a few days, Bailey had gone from an old but healthy dog to a sickly frail animal who panted with the slightest exertion and coughed when she barked. And the tumor in her cheek was now the size of a golf ball and distorting her face. She wouldn't eat dog food anymore, or even scrambled eggs. Now the only thing she would eat was raw hamburger mixed with bread and milk.

They were out of milk, so in the evening, Maya and Rhodes and Bailey walked down to the convenience store on the corner. Even this walk of two blocks left Bailey wheezing.

"I'll wait outside with her," Maya said.

Rhodes went into the store and Bailey flopped down on the sidewalk. A little white fluffy dog was leashed to the bike rack, but Bailey didn't go over to sniff her.

Maya knew that dog by sight, as well as the dog's owner, a fiftyish woman, who was presumably in the store. They lived in the neighborhood, and could be seen going for walks and running errands in all sorts of winds and weathers. Maya thought the dog's owner was probably single because she had never seen the woman with anyone else (or without the dog).

The dog's owner and Rhodes came out of the convenience store at the same time, and the little white dog danced around happily.

The woman looked at the dog, and said, "I love you."

She didn't say it in high, excited dog-speak. She said it exactly the way a woman might say it to her husband or lover. Maya and Rhodes looked at each other.

On the way home, walking slowly, slowly, for Bailey, Rhodes put his arm around Maya and she leaned against his side.

"At least," she said, "I'll never become that kind of person now."

Rhodes was thoughtful. "I wouldn't mind being that kind of person," he said.

That was Rhodes. He honestly wouldn't mind; she would. Did they complement each other or were they doomed? Maya could never figure it out.

· ·

Rhodes was gone on Thursday nights, so he could attend the project status review in Arlington for his department on Fridays (he worked with computers, and was an assistant professor, but that was actually as deep as Maya's knowledge of what he did went). This Thursday, Maya took a bubble bath and put on her blue kimono with the design of flying black gulls.

Then she sat at her computer, and Bailey curled up under the desk, where Maya could bury her bare toes in Bailey's fur. Maya drank two glasses of red wine and searched iTunes for songs about dying dogs, but all she could find was a track of Grandpa Jones singing "Old Blue." She downloaded it and put it on continuous repeat on the iPod docking station and sat on the couch, drinking a third glass of wine and stroking Bailey's head, which rested in her lap.

The doorbell rang, and Bailey made the sad coughing sound that was her bark now. Maya held the top of her kimono closed and went to answer it, still carrying her wineglass.

It was her boss, Gildas-Joseph, holding a heavy-looking nylon bag.

"Hello, Maya," he said. "I brought the tent we talked about."

Had they talked about a tent? Yes, she supposed they had. She and Rhodes wanted to go camping.

"Well, thank you so much," she said. He was obviously waiting for her to take the tent, but Maya didn't want the top of her robe to fall open, so she had to direct him around in a lady-of-the-manor sort of way, saying, "Just put it there in the corner, please," and gesturing with the hand that held the wineglass.

Gildas-Joseph put the tent down and then petted Bailey. "How is this old girl?" he said to her. "Hmmm? How are you?"

Maya blinked back tears. She suddenly felt very close to Gildas-Joseph. "Would you like a glass of wine?" she asked.

"I can't," Gildas-Joseph said. "My wife and children are in the car."

His wife and children were in the car! Maya suddenly felt like she'd offered him something illegal, or at least immoral. She reverted back to her regal mode, and said, "Well, thank you for stopping by," and balancing her wineglass with some difficulty on top of the shoe rack, she shook his hand.

He left and she imagined him getting into the car and saying to his wife, *Maya said she was too busy to write the Libri Foundation grant and there she is getting drunk in her bathrobe!*

Well, let him say that. Maya found she didn't care.

She drank the rest of the bottle of wine and most of another and passed out on the couch. When she woke up in the morning, she had a crick in her neck, her tongue felt like it had grown fur, and she thought she might have low-grade brain damage from listening to Grandpa Jones all night. But Bailey was licking her hand, and Maya realized that she did, amazingly, feel a little bit happier.

Hazelene stopped by at lunchtime with two Middle Eastern platters from the deli and a marrowbone from the butcher. She and Maya ate the Middle Eastern platters but Bailey only sniffed the marrowbone and then lay down next to it, thumping her tail against the floor a few times.

"I'm afraid she doesn't feel up to eating much," Maya said apologetically. She thought of how Bailey used to devote herself to getting every last bit of marrow out of bones, how she would spend all afternoon maneuvering the bone around with her nose and scraping with her teeth, making that particular *clunk-clunk* sound of a dog with a bone. Nothing else makes that sound.

But Hazelene was made of sterner stuff. She got a teaspoon from the kitchen and lay down on the carpet next to Bailey and fed her tiny spoonfuls of marrow. "Here you go," she said softly, encouragingly. "Isn't that good? Aren't you a lucky dog?"

When Bailey wouldn't take any more marrow, Hazelene still lay next to her, stroking her softly. Maya carried everything into the kitchen and threw the teaspoon in the trash because even though it could be put through the dishwasher and sterilized, she did not want to wonder every morning as she ate her yogurt whether she was using a spoon from which a dog with mouth cancer had eaten.

Then she realized that Hazelene and certainly Rhodes himself would feel the opposite. They would be proud to eat yogurt with Bailey's teaspoon, probably even before it had gone through the dishwasher. This thought made Maya cry (very quietly into a dish towel) because Rhodes, his mother, Bailey—they all deserved someone so much better.

Dr. Drummond called while Maya was in the shower, and left a message, saying he was calling to see how she and Bailey were. Maya knew that Dr. Drummond did not call all his clients and ask after their well-being, and part of her found this message meaningful and flattering, and part of her just felt impatient. She wanted to call him back and say, *Look, my dog is dying and my relationship may be ending, so if you want to get involved with me, let's just tell each other our stories and see how we go.*

Because Maya had a theory that everyone had a story that somehow defined them, both the good and the bad, and that these stories should be shared early on in relationships. If the other person appreciated the story, that meant you could proceed with the relationship, and if the other person failed to under-stand the depth of the story, or were judgmental, then there was basically no point in further contact. She thought of them as litmus-test stories.

Maya's own such story was that when she was twenty, she had an affair with an overweight economics professor and the one time they had sex with him on top, he was so heavy he actu-ally bruised one of Maya's ribs and when she cried, "Wait! Stop! I think you just broke my rib," the economics professor said, "I haven't finished yet."

It was a short anecdote, but Maya found it rich in nuance and meaning. She had once told this to a man she was dating and the man had attempted to *explain* the story to her, saying, "What he meant was—" and Maya had nearly shouted, "I know what he meant! It's the fact that he said it!" (Needless to say, she never saw that man again, and she never saw the economics professor again either, outside of class.)

Rhodes's litmus-test story, which he had told Maya about six weeks into their relationship, was that in high school, his friend Vince Brandigan had slept over and the next morning while Rhodes was in the shower, Hazelene had come up to the bed-room to see what they wanted for breakfast. When she knocked, Vince had shouted "Come in!" and when she opened the door, he was on the bed, masturbating, and obviously had been waiting for her. And although Hazelene had requested after this that Vince no longer visit, Rhodes remained friends with him through most of high school, and had in fact only *stopped* being friends with him after Vince made the football team and they didn't have much in common anymore. (A fascinating addendum to this story was that Vince was not only Rhodes's friend but a *neighbor* and his parents still lived about four blocks away from Rhodes's parents.

Vince himself presumably still came home to visit his parents, but sadly Maya had never seen him even though she made Rhodes drive slowly past the Brandigans' house near major holidays.)

Really, this story said everything about Rhodes, didn't it? Why Maya might want to leave him, why she might stay forever. And actually it also said quite a bit about Hazelene, and made it literally impossible to think about anything else when you saw her after you heard it the first time.

Maya had her recurring nightmare about marrying Rhodes, the one that made her wake up, gasping and panicky. Nothing would calm her except to wake Rhodes, who didn't mind. He didn't need much sleep and he said he liked being awake in the middle of the night.

So she shook Rhodes's shoulder, and said, "I had a bad dream."

"Again?" Rhodes said sleepily. He never asked what her bad dreams were about, which was just as well.

But he came around quickly and made them cups of tea and they sat up in bed and watched *Jeopardy!* on the television. At one point Alex Trebek said that the three occupations who did best on the show were lawyers, teachers, and librarians.

"Hey, maybe that'll be me someday," Maya said.

"You!" Rhodes hooted. "I can hear you now. 'I'll take Curling Irons for four hundred, Yeast Infections for a thousand.'"

Maya laughed and they put the TV on mute and discussed her potential top *Jeopardy!* categories, which also included Scented Candles, Stephen King, True Crime, and Naps, with a daily double of Famous Women Scientists (that last one was a bit of a surprise, but she had once designed a website for the Women in Science wing of a museum).

By then Maya was calm again, and she and Rhodes made love, and Maya slid back under the covers while Rhodes got up and worked on his laptop. She felt happy, and secure, and relaxed. It was somewhat counterintuitive, considering her dream. But Maya had never really, consistently, thought her relationship with Rhodes made the least bit of sense at all.

Maya took Bailey back to Dr. Drummond, because Bailey would eat nothing now but a mush made of bread and milk, and the tumor in her cheek was almost the size of a grapefruit. Maya sometimes thought she could actually see it getting bigger.

Dr. Drummond sat on the floor with Bailey again and opened her mouth to look in with his light. Bailey struggled, so Maya sat on the floor, too, and helped hold her still.

Dr. Drummond examined Bailey's mouth for a long time. Then he snapped off the light and looked at Maya. "The tumor is obstructing her throat now," he said. "She can't swallow very well and soon she'll have trouble breathing."

Maya tightened her grip on Bailey's collar.

"I think in the next day or two, it will be time," Dr. Drummond said.

"Time!" Maya said. Her voice squeaked. "But I thought you said two weeks! Before that they said *six* weeks!"

"I know," Dr. Drummond said quietly. He didn't seem to mind her blaming him. "It's more aggressive than we thought."

"But forty-eight hours . . . ," Maya began. It was such a short time. She wanted to argue him out of it.

"Think about it," Dr. Drummond said gently. He put his hand between her shoulder blades and let it rest there. "Tomorrow or the next day. After that we're into the weekend, and she won't make it through until next Monday. I know you don't want Bailey to suffer. I can come to your house and do it there, if you think Bailey would like that better."

Maya nodded because she didn't trust herself to speak.

Dr. Drummond gave Bailey another painkiller shot and some sort of very soft dog biscuit. He told Maya to call when she'd made a decision, and offered to walk her to her car again, but Maya shook her head.

She went out to her car and helped Bailey into the passenger seat. Then Maya got in on the driver's side, but she did not start the car right away. She was thinking that someday, possibly very soon, she would be a single, carefree, mellow, dogless person, able to date full professors and vets and whomever else she wanted. She wished this thought made her happy. She wished she could feel anything other than the purest, most leaden, darkest gray kind of sorrow.

That night, Rhodes's parents and Magellan brought over a home-made lasagna, some salad, and a bottle of wine. "I figured you probably didn't feel up to cooking much," Hazelene said.

Maya looked at the food, and then at their expectant faces. "You should join us."

Rhodes was walking through the kitchen, and he stopped, scratching his stomach beneath his T-shirt. "Doesn't it, like, counteract the helpfulness of bringing us dinner if you stay to eat it?" he asked. Rhodes said this kind of wildly negative thing in front of his parents all the time, which they either didn't get or were used to by now.

So the five of them crowded around the table and ate the lasagna. Hazelene ate with her right hand, and stroked Bailey's head with her left. "Bailey, Bailey," she said. Then she looked at Maya. "You know, I don't think I ever asked you why you named Bailey that."

"Because my favorite drink at that time was Baileys Irish Cream," Maya said. Then she added, "I was only eighteen."

She meant, *I was only eighteen, that's why I had such pathetic taste in alcohol,* but it sort of sounded like, *I was only eighteen, I drink much harder stuff now.*

"Oh, I love Baileys," Hazelene said. "At Christmastime, I pour some in a decanter and keep it in the front hall on a tray with some pretty little red liqueur glasses, and every time I pass by, I have a glass."

"Every time you pass by!" Magellan exclaimed. "Aren't you shit-faced by noon?"

"Hey, now," Desmond said. "What kind of language is that?"

(Which caused Maya, who was thinking there might be a glimmer of hope for Magellan after all, to quickly switch her train of thought and wonder how many times she'd sworn in front of Rhodes's father.)

Hazelene didn't seem upset by any of this. She was still stroking Bailey's face. "She's ten," she said. "Which is, what, eighty in dog years? And she's been healthy for almost all of it. I want to go like that, healthy right up to the end, and I don't want to live past eighty, anyway."

"If you like, we can make an appointment with the vet," Rhodes said. "We'll just tell him to stop by your house on September seventeenth, twenty-four years from now, and put you to sleep. We'll say, 'She may protest a little, but just ignore that.'"

Hazelene just looked at Maya and shook her head. Maya smiled. And suddenly it occurred to her that she had the relationship with Hazelene that she'd always hoped she'd have with

Rhodes's sister. She and Hazelene were friends, real friends, with the kind of friendship that made Maya think, as she sometimes did, that people were not meant to keep moving, that the world was actually a much better place when people lived in the same village their whole lives. She wished that she knew Hazelene in some other way, from work or the gym or the neighborhood, so that she could still have Rhodes's mother when she no longer had Rhodes himself.

The next day at the library, Maya called the veterinary clinic and made an appointment for Dr. Drummond to come over the following morning.

Then she called Rhodes and told him. He said, "But tomorrow is Friday, and I have to be at the status review."

"I know," Maya said. "But we have to do it soon, before she has trouble breathing."

"I don't want you to have to go through this without me," Rhodes said. "I don't want Bailey to have to go through it without me, either."

Suddenly Maya could barely breathe. Certainly Bailey would want Rhodes there. But it was too late now.

"It's okay," she said finally. "It would be harder for me if you were there. This way I have to be brave for Bailey."

She wanted it to be her and Bailey at the end, the way it had been her and Bailey in the beginning, so that someday, if she needed to, she could pretend Rhodes was just a minor blip on the radar somewhere in between.

After she hung up with Rhodes, she walked across the hall to Gildas-Joseph's office and told him that she would be taking the next day off because she had to have her dog put to sleep.

Gildas-Joseph's face clouded with concern and he had Maya come into his office and gave her a glass of pastis, which Maya drank, not because she liked pastis, or even needed it, but because she liked being in Gildas-Joseph's office with the door shut.

She realized that she was, in effect, using her dying dog to get dates with two different men. She thought there could be no doubt about it now. She was a horrible, horrible person.

In the morning, Bailey would eat nothing, not even when Maya tried to feed her with a teaspoon.

Dr. Drummond was not due to come until ten o'clock and Maya wanted to make this last hour with Bailey count, make it meaningful, but she and Bailey could only stare at each other. Maya realized that their two main forms of interaction were Maya taking Bailey for a walk, and Bailey trying to extort food from her, and now Bailey didn't feel well enough to do either of those things.

Eventually, Maya sat on the floor and Bailey lay down next to her. Maya watched a cooking show on television and stroked the pale fur on Bailey's side until her fingers were numb.

At ten to ten, Dr. Drummond arrived. He wore jeans and his white coat and a blue shirt that matched his eyes. Bailey got all excited and turned around in a clumsy circle and licked his hand. Maya knew this was because Bailey associated Dr. Drummond with the dog biscuit that he gave her at the end of the past visit, and wondered if it was disloyal to think on this, the last day of Bailey's life, that Bailey was actually kind of a dope to remember only the biscuit and not the shot.

"Come in," she said to Dr. Drummond. "We were just watching TV." She understood a second too late that this made her sound slightly demented. "I mean, I was. Bailey was just lying there."

But Dr. Drummond had bent over to pet Bailey and looked up and smiled gently. "I knew what you meant."

Maya supposed he encountered all sorts of dog-owner relations when he made house calls. "So," she said. "What do we do?"

"Just have Bailey lie down someplace where she's comfortable," Dr. Drummond said.

"Bailey, come here," Maya called, going back to the place where they had been sitting on the floor together. But Bailey chose this moment to be disobedient and went to the back door instead. "Oh, I think she wants to go out," Maya said.

"That's all right." Dr. Drummond smiled.

So Bailey went out and had a slow ramble around the backyard while Maya and Dr. Drummond had a stilted discussion about what a bad book *The Da Vinci Code* was and Maya wondered if she would someday be forced to look back on this as their first date.

"Does Bailey have a blanket or towel?" Dr. Drummond asked. "Something she could lie on?"

Maya went to the laundry room and got an old beach towel and brought it back and spread it out on the carpet. While she was doing that, Bailey came back to the door and Dr. Drummond let her in. Maya sat on the towel and Bailey came over and lay down next to her. Dr. Drummond opened his bag and took out a syringe.

"This will make her sleepy," he said, and then he knelt and gave Bailey the shot.

"It's okay," Maya said soothingly to Bailey, although in fact Bailey hadn't seemed to mind. Bailey licked the spot on her leg where he'd injected her and then put her head in Maya's lap. The shot worked amazingly fast; within a minute Bailey was snoring.

"Now we wait ten minutes to make sure she's asleep," Dr. Drummond said. He looked at his watch.

They did not speak while they waited. There was no sound but Bailey's snoring. Maya could not decide later if those ten minutes were very quick or very slow. She knew only that something had happened to time; it had changed, or maybe softened.

Dr. Drummond took another syringe from his bag. "This one will stop her heart." He looked apologetic. "She might wake up, or be agitated for a second."

Maya nodded.

Dr. Drummond sank the needle into Bailey's leg, and Maya stroked Bailey's head gently, over and over. But Bailey did not wake. She took a deep breath and did not let it out.

Dr. Drummond used his stethoscope to listen to Bailey's heart, and then he opened one of her eyelids and pressed her eyeball with his finger. He nodded. "Even dying, she was a good girl," he said softly.

And if Maya, who was an auditory person, had expected to hear something—distant church bells or the *whoosh* of Bailey's soul departing—she was mistaken. She could hear only the dripping of the kitchen faucet, and the chugging of the dishwasher, and the faint sounds of people on the street outside, going on with their lives.

Dr. Drummond wrapped Bailey's body in the towel and carried it out to his van. He put it carefully in the back. He would take her to be cremated and bring her ashes back to Maya at some point.

She stood next to his van and watched as he closed the door. "Are you okay?" he asked.

She nodded.

Dr. Drummond put his arm around her, and then held her for a moment. He smelled faintly like disinfectant, faintly like dog. Again, Maya knew that he probably did not embrace all his clients, knew this should be a significant moment, but she felt numb. Was she really standing here, hugging the vet? Was Bailey's body really in the back of that van? Was the sun really shining so brightly?

After Dr. Drummond drove away, Maya went inside. She sent Rhodes a text, saying: *It's over. Please don't call because I'll start crying if I hear your voice.* It occurred to her that this was a text that she could send him if she broke up with him, that it would also apply then. Because it was easy to imagine leaving him when he wasn't around, but nearly impossible to contemplate when he was.

She unloaded the dishwasher and put some laundry in the washing machine. She took out the garbage and made a shopping list. She could do this. She could. She put Bailey's dishes and leash in a shoe box and put the shoe box on the top shelf of the closet.

Then she made herself a cup of coffee and sat down at her desk. She slipped off her shoes and automatically stretched out her feet to rest them on Bailey.

After a moment, Maya pulled her heels up onto the chair and leaned her head against her knees and cried. She cried because Bailey would never again lie under her desk while she worked. Bailey would never again make her feel safe on Thursday nights while Rhodes was away. Bailey would never again make an anguished sob when Maya took too long putting on her coat before a walk. Maya cried about all these things. But mainly she cried because the world had been nicer when Bailey came into it, and now Bailey was gone.

Maya was taking a bubble bath when Rhodes got home. A dozen tiny scented candles were burning in the bathroom and a glass of wine rested on the floor near the tub.

She heard the door open and close downstairs and the sounds of Rhodes moving around, opening his mail, getting a drink. He called up to her but she didn't answer.

After a little while, he came into the bathroom.

"Hey," he said.

"Hey," Maya said back, softly.

He sat on the edge of the tub. He reached for her hand under the water, and held it. He did not seem to mind that his sleeve got wet, just the way he wouldn't have minded about eating from the dog-teaspoon.

Rhodes ran his free hand through his hair. "The house seemed so empty when I got home," he said. Then he sighed. "The world became a bleaker place today."

This was so close to what Maya had thought earlier that she could only stare at him. She sat up slightly in the tub and gripped his hand harder. It seemed to her that all the candle flames leapt up at the same time and burned more brightly for a moment.

Maya knew then that she could not leave Rhodes. Bailey's death had prevented it, the same way that a flat tire or broken alarm clock could prevent someone from making a flight that later crashed.

There is such a thing as too much loss. Maya understood that now.

BLUE HERON BRIDGE

The worst thing about the affair, Nina thought, was that it made her so impatient with the children. She had not thought that would be the worst part. She thought the guilt would be the worst thing, or the stress of constant deception, or falling out of love with her husband, or some awful day of reckoning, but so far none of these things had happened. Only the impatience.

And they were great children, two little girls, Jane and Chloe, eight and six. Sweet, bright, lively, healthy girls. When Nina was pregnant, she swore that if she could just have children like these, she would never, ever ask for anything else. And now she had them, and suddenly they drove her crazy.

Her husband, Hamish, drove her crazy, too, as did her friends and neighbors and coworkers. The only person besides David who did not irritate Nina was her sixteen-year-old stepdaughter, Francesca, and that was ironic since Nina sometimes had a hard time coping when Francesca came from England to spend the summer. But not this year. This year, Francesca was infinitely bearable, and Nina knew it was because she and Francesca were the same age emotionally now.

Oh, it was horrible to have a teenager's emotions and a forty-year-old's body. It was humiliating. It was depressing. It was degrading. It made her feel alive to the very tips of her toes.

· ·

The affair was not Nina's fault, or so she later decided. It was more the result of a random series of events. She and Hamish had moved to Riviera Beach to be in a better school district, and now the office where Nina worked three days a week as a medical librarian was twenty miles away, too far to go by bicycle. Before, they had lived eight miles away, and she could handle riding her bike sixteen miles in the Florida heat, but she couldn't handle forty. She would have to find a new way to exercise.

She decided on running and bought new running shoes and two pairs of Lycra running pants and two shirts, one in black and one in beige, and two high-impact sports bras. (She realized afterward that this was the best part of running, buying the clothes, and wished she'd spent longer doing it.)

After dinner that first night in mid-June, she had left Hamish with the girls, put on her new clothes and shoes, and stepped outside.

"Oh, hello, Nina," said her next-door neighbor, Bunny Pringle, from her porch.

Bunny Pringle was an extremely social, somewhat overweight blonde about Nina's age, married to a city commissioner, and with children the same age as Nina's. She seemed to be on her porch more or less permanently, drinking iced tea, and spoke to Nina whenever Nina entered or left the house. She was always inviting Nina to parties, all-female parties, where they did some activity, like scrapbooking or jewelry making or Indian cooking. Nina never went. The most interesting thing about Bunny Pringle, in Nina's opinion, was that everyone always referred to her by both her first and last name, like Darth Vader.

"Hello," Nina said now.

"Are you going running?" Bunny Pringle said. "I admire you. Do you know David, who lives around the corner? He's a personal trainer and ran the Miami marathon last year."

"Well, I'm just a beginner," Nina said.

She started running down the block. She hadn't gotten very far when she realized that her legs, nicely muscled from years of cycling, could have probably run the Miami marathon, too, but she began to doubt that her lungs could make it to the corner store.

She had planned to run three miles, having picked that number arbitrarily, but after half a mile, she turned and ran home. She would have liked to walk, but she knew Bunny Pringle would be watching, and probably lots of other people, too. (It was that kind of neighborhood.)

So she jogged up to her house, waved at Bunny Pringle, opened the door, staggered in, and lay on the living room carpet, panting.

"Jesus," Francesca said, stepping over her with a bowl of ice cream. "Have some self-respect."

Today David's wife had to work late and his children were in day care, so the afternoon was theirs, if Nina could find someone to watch Jane and Chloe. Francesca was working at the Dairy Queen, so Nina rushed the girls over to Bunny Pringle's.

"Of course I don't mind having the girls for a few hours," Bunny Pringle said. "My kids will love it. Go on down to the playroom, girls. Actually, Nina, I was going to ask *you* a favor."

"Sure thing," said Nina, who had already turned to go.

"Well, I'm sure you know that the minister from our church, Reverend McWilliams, has been staying in our guest bedroom for a few months since the parsonage flooded," Bunny Pringle said.

"Oh, yes," Nina said. She didn't know that, or didn't remember, or didn't care. Probably all three.

"I'm afraid it's a delicate situation," Bunny Pringle continued, "but we're redecorating that room in Vivienne Westwood Absence of Rose. Do you know what that looks like? I can get the book and show you."

"That's all right." Nina felt she might physically harm Bunny Pringle if she had to stand there and listen to any more of this drivel while David waited seven houses away. "What's the favor?"

Bunny Pringle looked a little startled to have it put so bluntly. "Well, the decorators are scheduled to come next week. Could Reverend McWilliams stay with you for a week or so? I know it's a lot to ask, but—"

"No problem," Nina said hastily. "Call me later with the details. I really have to fly now. Thanks for everything, Bunny!"

And Nina was off to David's house, and then back to her own house to shower, and frantically throw together dinner, and send Francesca to pick up the girls and buy milk, and it wasn't until much later that evening that Bunny Pringle called and Nina remembered her promise.

Afterward, she went into the living room where Hamish was reading the paper and Jane and Chloe were lying on the floor, watching TV.

"Hamish," Nina said slowly. "I'm sorry to do this without checking with you first, but a Presbyterian minister is going to be staying with us for a few weeks." (The time seemed to have magically expanded since the first time she spoke to Bunny Pringle.)

Hamish put down the paper and stared at her. "Holy shit."

"I don't think you should say that in front of him," Nina said.

"Why the hell would a Presbyterian minister want to stay with us?"

Could he not utter a single sentence without swearing? "I'm not sure he *wants* to that all-fired much," Nina said. "It's just that I told Bunny Pringle he could."

Hamish opened the paper again. "Okay," he said. "Maybe I can help him with his sermons." Hamish was an atheist.

Chloe turned on her side. "He's not going to sleep in my room, is he?"

"No, honey, he'll sleep in the bedroom over the garage," Nina said, relieved that everyone seemed to be accepting the news.

"I hope he doesn't mind the musty smell," Jane said, without taking her eyes off the TV.

"We'll air it out," Nina said.

"*I* hope he doesn't mind daddy longlegs," said Chloe, "because there are, like, two hundred million of them out there."

"We'll spray, I guess," Nina said.

"Maybe he'll *pray* the spiders away," Hamish said.

"Where's he going to shower, though?" Jane said. "Do we have to see him in his bathrobe?"

"God, you guys!" Nina snapped. "We'll figure it out, okay? You don't have to obsess over every little detail."

She turned and went upstairs, past her own room, to Francesca's, and looked out the window. This was the only window from which she could see David's house, and even from here, she could see only a tiny portion of the peaked roof and an attic vent. But she could see it, and it belonged to David, and it was like honey to her soul.

During the first few weeks of summer, Nina's lung capacity had increased, and she was able to run two miles, sometimes two and a half, without stopping. One evening she ran three miles but was forced to walk the last few blocks home. A man wearing cutoff jeans was out, watering his lawn, and as Nina walked by, he said, "How do you like running?" proving her suspicion that all the neighbors watched her.

"I love it," Nina said promptly. Privately, she felt that her mind and body had bifurcated, and that her mind was determined she would run, and her body was like some reluctant old horse being flogged over a jump. She wasn't sure yet which would triumph.

"I'm David," the man said, holding out his hand.

"Oh, Bunny Pringle's friend," Nina said, shaking hands with him. He gave her an odd look, so she said quickly, "I'm sorry, I'm sure you have more depth than that. I mean, more of an identity." Now it seemed she was *becoming* Bunny Pringle, saying things that didn't really make sense, but David just nodded. He was in his late thirties, with dark curly hair and the deep, even tan of a long-term Florida resident.

"How fast do you run?" he asked. "How many minutes per mile?"

"I have no idea," said Nina, who knew exactly. "But *slow* is probably the best word for it. Last week an elderly man in bedroom slippers passed me."

David laughed and looked at her, and Nina got the sense she sometimes got when she said something funny, that she had suddenly become visible.

David continued watering his lawn. "Maybe we should go running together," he said.

"Yes," she said slowly. "I would like that."

And so Nina and David had begun running every evening. The first night, he told her about a seventy-five-year-old man who was suspected of having cheated and taken the Tube during the London marathon, or otherwise the man had suddenly begun running three-minute miles, and Nina laughed and nearly stumbled into someone's flower bed.

So after that she told David that he couldn't say anything funny while they ran, and he didn't, but sometimes he would take a breath as though he were *about* to say something, and Nina would start laughing.

"How can you laugh when I don't say anything?" David asked.

"I don't know," Nina said, and it was true. But his silences intrigued her. Everything about him intrigued her.

Now she could run five miles, from the corner by David's house, across the Blue Heron Bridge, and back. She liked going over the bridge best, where there was a slight breeze and she and David always each touched one foot on the far side and then reversed direction, like runners in a relay race.

"Are you going to the block party this weekend?" David asked one night, as they ran back across the bridge.

There was a block party scheduled for Saturday, arranged by Bunny Pringle, of course. "Yes," Nina said. "Are you?"

"Yes," David said.

And they ran on, in silence. Nina thought they had so much not to say to each other, it was amazing.

The first dinner with Reverend McWilliams was successful, in Nina's opinion, not because of what happened, but because of what *didn't*.

No one snickered or said anything inappropriate when Reverend McWilliams, a thin man with sandy hair and glasses, asked if they could say grace before the meal. Chloe, whose best friend,

Grace Abbot, had been away at dyslexia camp all summer, even echoed "Grace!" in a soft wondering voice, which made her sound very enthusiastic. Reverend McWilliams suggested that they all say grace silently, each praising God for their blessings, and everyone managed to be quiet for thirty seconds until he said, "Amen."

Also, there were no long awkward silences, which Nina had feared. Reverend McWilliams was very talkative. He thanked them for having him and said he was sure he'd be extremely comfortable. (Nina held her breath but nobody mentioned spiders or the musty smell.) He also talked about Bunny Pringle and what a terrific person she was and how kind and generous and how she'd given him a clever little doodad that enabled him to remove the core from an apple and simultaneously cut the apple into six pieces.

"An apple divider?" Hamish said.

"You mean there's a *name* for it?" Reverend McWilliams asked, evidently having thought it was a one-of-a-kind device Bunny had whipped up in some hidden workshop.

Francesca talked about her job at Dairy Queen and did not refer to the manager as an asshole (it turned out he'd been absent that day), and she even offered to give Reverend McWilliams a free cone if he ever stopped by. Nina thought that was probably immoral, if not illegal, but Reverend McWilliams said he'd be delighted.

No one sighed or rolled her eyes when Hamish told the little girls that studies had shown they'd make more money from their lemonade stand if they asked for donations instead of charging a fixed rate, explaining the economic principle behind this. Reverend McWilliams even looked interested and said, "Tell me more," but Nina supposed that was something he'd been taught in seminary.

Oh, dinner went very well, but afterward things fell apart. Jane and Chloe ran off to watch *The Simpsons* without asking to be excused, and when Reverend McWilliams offered to help with the dishes, Francesca said breezily, "No, we play Hearts to see who does the dishes."

"Really?" Reverend McWilliams said. "Then I must take my chances and join in."

The Hearts games were a family tradition, developed long ago between her and Hamish and Francesca, but Nina had planned on excluding Reverend McWilliams. Instead, as she cleared the table, Francesca filled him in on all their personal rules, including that they played to fifty-eight, that being Hamish's age.

"Unless you're even older than *that*," she said in an offhand way, probably offending both Hamish and Reverend McWilliams.

Reverend McWilliams was a much better cardplayer than Nina had suspected, and she was relieved to find that she would not have to intentionally lose to spare herself the humiliation of forcing a clergyman to wash the dishes. It was, in fact, Francesca who lost and Reverend McWilliams who gave her the queen of spades on the last hand, pushing her score up to sixty-four.

"Oh, *fock*," Francesca said, the slight mispronunciation making the swearword seem even worse to Nina.

"Francesca," she said gently.

"What?" Francesca said, puzzled. "He *queened* me, in case you didn't notice." She shoved back her chair and got up and began running water in the sink.

Nina closed her eyes, too ashamed to look at Reverend McWilliams. She had brought this on herself, she knew, in many ways, not the least of which was that during grace, when they were all supposed to be silently thankful for their blessings, she had been thankful for David.

· ·

Nina had spent more than an hour getting ready for the block party. She did her makeup carefully and wore her melon-colored sheath and her wedge heels and her gold hoop earrings. Her hair was auburn and wavy and she pulled it into a side ponytail so that it tumbled over one shoulder. She was perfectly satisfied with her reflection in the mirror.

But when she came downstairs and found Hamish and the little girls waiting for her (Francesca was at work), she realized that dating, if that's what she and David were doing, was easier when you were single and had to make only yourself, not your whole family, presentable.

Jane and Chloe had been playing with Francesca's makeup and now sported frosted lip gloss and blue eye shadow. They looked a lot like child prostitutes. Plus, Chloe had a big chocolate-ice-cream stain on the front of her blouse. Hamish had not shaved, and the lower half of his face was covered with grizzled stubble. He was wearing an ancient shirt so full of holes around the collar that it was almost two separate garments. Hamish frequently looked like this on weekends, and once when they were camping he had gone off looking for firewood and some woman had mistaken him for a wino and yelled at him to get off her campsite. That was one of Nina's fondest memories, but today she was filled only with irritation.

"Change clothes and wash off that makeup, girls," she said, making her voice brisk. (They stared at her as though she weren't speaking English.) "And, Hamish, can't you wear a different shirt?"

"I could, but I don't want to," Hamish said.

After much negotiation, Nina got Chloe to change, but the

girls refused to wash off the makeup. Hamish put on a fresh shirt, which only made him look like a homeless person trying to make a new start in life. Nina looked at them all and sighed.

But in the end, what did it really matter? David was at the party but didn't speak to her, didn't even look at her. He stayed near the keg, balancing his younger child, a toddler, on his shoulder and talking to a group of men from farther down the block whom Nina didn't know. His wife, someone said, was a pediatrician and on call this weekend, so Nina didn't meet her, either. Jane and Chloe realized that traffic had been blocked off and ran back home for their bikes, and Nina didn't see them again. Hamish spent the entire party talking about prime-number factorization to a tax lawyer from a few houses down, and Nina was forced to sit at a picnic table with Bunny Pringle and listen while Bunny debated the pros and cons of getting a guinea pig.

Had there ever been such an anticlimactic evening, except maybe that time in college when Nina's professor had insisted they have a conference to discuss her comparative lit paper late at night in his office, and they had actually discussed the paper? (Nina had spent a long time on her makeup that night, too.)

Eventually, Nina managed to extricate herself from Bunny Pringle and went to find Hamish to tell him she was going home, and as she approached him—"Public key encryption hangs from the prime-number factorization theorem by a thread," Hamish was saying—the crowd shifted slightly, and Nina saw David. He was watching Hamish, studying him in a cold, measuring, competitive way. It was a look of intense dislike, which Nina recognized instantly because she would have disliked David's wife with the same intensity, had she shown up to be disliked.

Nina turned abruptly and left the party without telling Hamish. She hardly slept that night.

• •

On the days Nina worked from the office, she dropped Jane and Chloe at a day camp, and Hamish left work early to pick them up. But tonight, as Nina packed the girls' lunches for the next day, Hamish said, "Could you get Jane and Chloe tomorrow, Francesca?"

Francesca was looking through a magazine at the table where Hamish sat drinking a glass of wine. "No, I work the evening shift tomorrow."

Hamish turned to Nina. "Can you get a sitter? Because I have to go to Caroline's house for drinks after work."

Caroline was his secretary. "If you're going over to a twenty-six-year-old woman's apartment for drinks," Nina said, amused, "don't you think the least you can do is arrange the sitter yourself?" Then she stopped, suddenly remembering that infidelity was not something they could joke about anymore. Or should.

"It's not like that," Hamish said. "The whole department's going. She's having a housewarming. Besides, I wouldn't have an affair with my secretary."

"Why not?" Francesca asked.

"It's too predictable," Hamish told her. "It's a cliché."

"Plus, I'm sure she's not remotely interested in you," Francesca said, flipping a page of her magazine.

He looked offended. "Why not?"

"Oh, please," Francesca said. "Like she'd be *so* fascinated to know Jesus had a little brother."

"*Twin* brother," Hamish said. "And you found it interesting enough to remember, even if incorrectly."

Nina scraped the carrot peelings down the garbage disposal

and flipped the switch. David was two years younger than Nina, making him twenty years younger than Hamish, and that bothered Nina sometimes, because it did seem like a cliché, the wife having an affair with a man more her age. (Oh, and the joy it would have given Hamish's first wife, who had long ago predicted such a thing!) It was odd, in the end, but Nina almost felt worse about the triteness of it than about anything else. Hamish deserved something more original.

Two days after the block party, Nina's phone rang at her office.

"It's me," David said.

If it had been anyone else, Nina would have said, "Who is this?" But she was afraid to tease him. She was afraid he might hang up. So all she said was "Yes."

In fact, all Nina said during the whole phone conversation was "Yes."

David asked if she could get away, he asked if she could meet him for a drink, he asked if she knew where the bar was, if she knew it was in a hotel, if she knew why he wanted to meet in a hotel, if she was okay with that.

"Yes," Nina said, gripping the phone so tightly her hand hurt. *Yes. Yes. Yes. Yes. Yes.*

They made love in the middle of the hotel room, standing up, David lifting her as though she weighed nothing at all. Nina thought the muscles on his shoulders were beautiful. "Isn't this killing your back?" she asked.

Hamish would have laughed, but David just shook his head. Apparently adultery was serious to him. Well, fair enough.

Afterward, David set her down on the dresser and brushed the hair out of her face. His expression was very solemn. "I've done this only once before," he said. "I mean, with one other person. You?"

"Never," Nina said. She kissed him, sucking gently on his lower lip. "I had been blind, and deaf, and sleeping; now, no longer."

David looked pleased, but Nina could tell he did not recognize the quote. He had not read *My Cousin Rachel,* which was Nina's favorite novel. She didn't even care.

It might seem as though it would be difficult to summon the moral fortitude to have an extramarital affair when a minister was living above your garage, but Nina had discovered that almost anything was possible. Actually, things were easier because now she could use Reverend McWilliams as a babysitter instead of Bunny Pringle.

"I'd be delighted to watch Jane and Chloe for you, Nina," he said whenever she asked. "What shall we do, girls?"

He seemed to think that watching them meant constantly interacting with them, or maybe he was just very conscientious. Jane and Chloe liked him, although Nina suspected that if they were even a little bit older, they would make fun of him.

So many experiences were new to him! It was like having an exchange student from Sudan, or maybe rural Scotland, someplace where people lead a very sheltered existence. Reverend McWilliams had never eaten risotto, or drunk Pimm's. He didn't know shampoo could cost forty dollars (Nina special-ordered it), and he jumped every time the GPS spoke in the car. He knew who Frank Sinatra was but not that he was dead, and he was entirely unaware that the Glastonbury Festival had taken place (here Francesca just shook her head, unable to comprehend the depth of his ignorance). He marveled at Hamish's collapsible bike and that Nina had special shoes just for running. He had never seen a Wii before, and he still hadn't played one, because Jane and Chloe liked him to be a spectator only. He had never watched *Jurassic Park,* not even the first one. ("Ask him why God lets nice people get eaten by velociraptors," Hamish told the girls, though Nina thought that might be too theoretical, even for a theologian.) He hadn't seen *SpongeBob SquarePants* or *The Simpsons,* he didn't know the difference between Miley Cyrus and Hannah Montana, and he seemed completely unable to hear or pronounce the *i* in *iCarly,* even after Jane wrote it out for him.

Bunny Pringle told Nina that Reverend McWilliams had been married but that his wife had died in the first year of their marriage, crushed between a tractor and a hay wagon on the church trip to a pumpkin patch. Nina did not know what to make of this. Would Reverend McWilliams be a more sophisticated person if his wife had lived? Had the world stopped for him in some elemental way on that long-ago Halloween? Had Mrs. McWilliams been the force that propelled the reverend through life? Would she have kept him from being passed from house to house like surplus homegrown zucchini?

He was a passionate cardplayer, and sometimes when they played Hearts to see who would wash the dishes, he and Francesca would crow victory or moan defeat so loudly that Nina had to shush them. Reverend McWilliams told Nina that these Hearts games were the most fun he'd had. Nina waited for him to add "this year" or "since the church softball game," but apparently he meant the most fun he'd *ever* had, which was kind of upsetting. Nina wondered if they would have to keep playing Hearts after Francesca went back to her mother's in late September. And how long was Reverend McWilliams going to stay, anyway? What if he never left? Why did he have to say "Go with God" every time someone left the house? On the whole, Nina decided, she would have preferred an exchange student from rural Scotland.

One day in early August they made love in David's car, on a dusty gravel road shaded by palm trees. When they finished, David turned on the engine so they could have air-conditioning and said, "I have to tell you something."

Nina was in the passenger seat, sweating, panting, her mind shattered by sexual pleasure. But something about his voice made her mind reassemble, like the cyborg in *Terminator 2,* the separate little pieces rolling back toward one another with a metallic clicking sound. She was afraid it wasn't coming back together fast enough.

"Okay," she said. Her mouth was dry.

David lifted his hips and slid his jeans back up and zipped them. Apparently this was something he had to tell her with his clothes on. Nina picked her underpants off the floor and slipped them on under her skirt.

David fingered his key ring. "You know I had another affair," he said. "I mean, I told you, and you said you never wanted to know the details."

"I still don't," Nina said quickly.

"But I feel like I have to tell you," he said. "Because it was someone you know."

Nina stared at him. "Who?"

He hesitated. "Bunny Pringle."

Nina kept staring. If he had said *Bunny,* she would have said *Bunny PRINGLE?* even though she was certain neither of them knew any other women named Bunny. Instead, she could only sit there horrified.

"She—" Nina began and stopped. Her brain was not cohesive enough for this conversation. She tried again. "She has a double chin."

She saw that unexpectedly she had scored a point. David looked ashamed.

"She collects *garden gnomes*," Nina said. "You had an affair with someone who collects garden gnomes."

David sighed. "I know there's that side of her," he said. "But I never saw that. I was in love with her, big-time—"

"Stop," Nina said. "I don't want to know anything else." But it turned out she did, because something occurred to her. "Except when it started and ended."

"It started last summer," David said. Again the hesitation. "And ended three weeks ago."

"Three weeks ago!" Nina brought her fingers to her mouth. "But you and I—"

"Yes," David said. "There was some overlap."

Nina turned from him and fumbled with the door handle. She stepped out. The heat knocked into her like an invisible punching bag. She wanted so much to leave David there and walk away, but how could she? The earth had shifted; it seemed unsteady under her feet. She didn't know where she could step, where the ground would take her weight. She leaned dizzily against the car and then dropped back into the passenger seat.

"You told me because she and I are neighbors, didn't you?" she said. "You were afraid we might confide in each other."

David said nothing.

"Take me home," she said. She wondered if home was still there, in such a changed world.

• •

Nina was miserable, more miserable than she had known it was possible to be. She could not eat, could not sleep, and she shivered constantly as though she had a fever. She told Hamish she was coming down with the flu, and he kept the girls out of her way as much as he could. She lost five pounds, something that ordinarily would have pleased her immensely, but she didn't care.

David called her cell phone constantly, but Nina kept the sound turned off and disabled her voice mail. He would only tell her, as he had in the car as he'd driven her home, that he loved her, that he'd told her because he didn't want there to be secrets between them, that he'd never meant to hurt her, that it was over between him and Bunny Pringle, that Bunny Pringle wouldn't even take his calls anymore. Nina didn't think she could survive if she had to hear that last phrase, and understand its implications, again.

Time went by so slowly, maybe because she hardly slept. At work they finished cataloging the cellular pathology section and ordered barbecued ribs to celebrate. Reverend McWilliams learned to play the Nintendo DS. Hamish made pot roast. Francesca got a reverse French manicure that made her hands look like clusters of red-tipped anemones. Nobody seemed to notice that Nina was shredded inside. Only one week had gone by since David had told her.

Nina got up late one night to make some tea. She heard footsteps, and a moment later Francesca joined her in the kitchen.

"Are you feeling better?" Francesca asked.

"A little," Nina said, touched that Francesca had noticed, had cared enough to ask.

But apparently it was just a brief sort of formality, or possibly a segue into talking about herself, because right away Francesca said, "Well, I'm totally nervous about going back to school next week" and launched into a long, complicated story about some girl named Missy Stevens who was unpopular but whose mother was friends with Francesca's mother and so couldn't be jettisoned in the normal manner, and Francesca was trying to walk the narrow line of being nice to Missy when no one else was around, but Missy kept trying to sit with her at lunch and stuff, and all Francesca could do was hope that over the summer Missy had found some other loser to hang out with—

Nina was leaning against the counter, drinking her tea, but suddenly she set her cup down and hugged Francesca.

"What?" Francesca said nervously. She and Nina had seldom embraced.

"Nothing," Nina said. She inhaled the orange-blossom shampoo scent of Francesca's hair. She thought that everyone should have a teenager to live with in times of heartbreak. They asked so little of you, really.

Now every interaction with Bunny Pringle was torturous. Well, truthfully, interactions with Bunny Pringle had *always* been torturous but now they were doubly so, exponentially so, because not only did Nina have to listen to whatever bit of random nonsense was drifting through Bunny Pringle's mind, she had to picture David and Bunny Pringle together while she did it.

Nina found that she almost literally could not see Bunny Pringle as a person but only as a sum of her parts, and she analyzed each part mercilessly. First, there were Bunny Pringle's eyes, which were okay, a nice pretty blue and very round. Her eyebrows were fairer than Nina's and, Nina decided, overplucked.

Her hair was honey blond and cut in a completely anonymous bob, with Dutch-girl bangs, which Nina had always disliked. Her skin was clear but tended to flush when she got excited. (Oh, but don't think about that—quick, think about something else.) Her nose was nondescript and her cheeks too full. Her body was too full also, but Nina could almost never get to Bunny Pringle's body because first she examined Bunny Pringle's mouth, and that was so upsetting. Bunny Pringle's mouth was pretty and rounded and a pale rose color even without lipstick, and Nina could not bear to think of that mouth kissing David's mouth, kissing David's body. Had Bunny Pringle's mouth, like Nina's, made the swift trail of butterfly kisses down David's chest and stomach? Had she—

It was better not to see Bunny Pringle than to think these things. But it was so hard to avoid her. Nina cleared out space in the garage so she could park the car there instead of in the driveway, close the garage door behind her, and enter the house using the back door. Because it seemed as if every time Nina left the house, even just to get the paper from the end of the drive, Bunny Pringle would hail her from her own porch.

Hi, Nina, how are things with Reverend McWilliams? . . . Have you seen the latest Twilight *movie? . . . Do you have a copy of* The Bridges of Madison County? *. . . Are you going to the farmers' market? Could you get me some corn? . . . I'm placing a Pampered Chef order, do you want anything?*

The pure inanity of the woman drove Nina crazy. How had David stood it? How had he endured her Pampered Chef parties, and her Christmas ornament exchanges, and her hen nights, and her garden club, and her candy tastings, and her cake-decorating lessons, and her fucking *antique thimble* collection?

Even outside her own neighborhood, Nina had to see her. She

drove to the supermarket with the girls, and as she pulled into a parking space, Chloe said, "Look, there's Mrs. Pringle."

So Nina looked. And there was Bunny Pringle, climbing out of her car, looking large in white painter pants and a flowery tunic. Nina swallowed. Was it possible, was it really possible, that she could sit here, her heart scraped raw with jealousy over a fat woman who scrapbooked? How had the world come to this?

"Why aren't we getting out of the car?" Jane asked. "Did you forget your purse?"

It was a minute before Nina could find her voice. "Yes, love," she said finally. "That's exactly what I did." And they drove home again.

One night they all went to the movies. Reverend McWilliams popped a bag of microwave popcorn to take with him.

"They sell that stuff at the theater, you know," Jane told him.

"Yes, I know, but this is far more economical," Reverend McWilliams said.

Francesca was brushing her hair in front of the hall mirror. "You have been to the movies before, right?" she asked.

"Yes, of course," Reverend McWilliams said.

Francesca glanced at Nina, a look so brief it was really no more than a flutter of Francesca's long lashes. "Just checking," she said and went back to brushing her hair.

Reverend McWilliams didn't get to eat his popcorn at the movies—Jane and Chloe ate it on the walk there. They said it smelled too good. So they walked together on the sidewalk, passing the paper bag back and forth between them. Reverend McWilliams and Francesca walked behind them and Francesca told Reverend McWilliams exactly how many calories there were in a Dairy Queen Blizzard. Nina and Hamish walked behind them and Nina thought that she should start a dating website that matched socially starved ministers with self-involved teen-age girls.

After the movie, they all walked home again and sat on the porch. (Bunny Pringle was absent from her porch, thankfully; she was inside, hosting a gift-wrapping party, Nina knew.) The little girls put on their swimsuits and turned on the sprinklers while the adults ate bowls of peppermint-stick ice cream. Hamish talked to them about quantum key cryptography and weak photon measurement until Francesca said, "Dad, do you, like, filter what you're going to say and wonder whether we're interested? Or is it that once something's on the launchpad, it has to come out?"

"I don't *wonder* whether you'll be interested," Hamish said. "I'm sure of it."

"Based on what, exactly?" Francesca asked.

On the lawn, the girls squealed and laughed and raced through the sprinkler again. Jane wore a pale blue swimsuit, Chloe a lime-green one, and their arms and legs were as smooth and tanned and unblemished as a bolt of brown velvet.

It was a perfect evening, really, except that Nina felt as if she might start sobbing and never stop.

Nina could not avoid Bunny Pringle forever. Bunny cornered her one morning at the coffee shop.

"Nina!" she said. "I haven't talked to you in ages! Can I sit with you?"

So Nina sighed and set aside her newspaper. Bunny sat down

and ordered a bagel with extra cream cheese and mint tea. Nina had only the mint tea; it seemed she had basically given up eating.

"So you won't believe who friended me on Facebook this morning," Bunny Pringle said.

Nina was thinking that Bunny Pringle's face was actually sort of bulbous looking if you tilted your head a certain way. "Who?"

"Reverend McWilliams!"

"Oh, that was Francesca," Nina said. "She set up an account for him and pretty much manages it. It took her, like, three hours to explain the concept to him and he still calls it Friendbook."

The whole family called it Friendbook now. Just the way they called the bread knife the "special knife" and their iPhones "portaphones." It was like having a two-year-old in the house again, except one that wasn't cute or related to them.

"We went ahead and got a guinea pig," Bunny Pringle said. "Her name is Lady and she eats sunflower seeds."

Nina waited, but no punch line or insight seemed to be forthcoming. "What's your point?" she asked finally.

Bunny seemed more thoughtful than offended. "Oh, just that your girls should come over and see her."

"Maybe," Nina said. "It doesn't sound that exciting, to be honest."

What was exciting was this new freedom to be rude to Bunny.

"Well—" Bunny began, but the waitress arrived with her bagel just then.

Bunny spread cream cheese on her bagel and then licked her knife. The gesture struck Nina as so complacent and unintelligent—the way a cow would lick medicine off a farmer's finger—that she had a sudden vicious urge to tell Bunny about her and David. She could picture the way Bunny's expression

would go from disbelief to belief, the way her chin would trem-
ble and then the rest of her face would crumple in on itself, like
Chloe's did when she broke something.

But Nina would never tell Bunny, not out of discretion, but
because it would make Nina and Bunny Pringle equals, it would
unite them in some sort of sisterhood of wronged women. It
would make them the same, and they were nothing alike. They
were different in every possible way. For instance, Nina was
never going to drink mint tea again.

Nina got up at seven the next morning and forced herself to eat a
banana. She wanted to go running. She went upstairs and dressed
in her running pants and black shirt and laced up her running
shoes.

When she walked back through the kitchen, Francesca and
Reverend McWilliams were sitting at the kitchen table, the rev-
erend in his bathrobe, Francesca in her Dairy Queen uniform.
Francesca's laptop was on the table between them, open to
Facebook.

"I still don't understand," Reverend McWilliams was saying.
"How does it make my life better to know that Bunny Pringle's
making corn muffins?"

Was there no escaping the woman?

"That's not really—" Francesca began.

"And yesterday she cleaned out the refrigerator," Reverend
McWilliams said. "I read that too."

Francesca sighed. "Look, she's a moron."

"Well," Reverend McWilliams said. "Not to put too fine a
point on it."

Nina touched Francesca's shoulder and said, "Stay until I get back, okay? The girls are sleeping."

"I can't," Francesca said. "I work the early shift and have to leave in ten minutes."

"I'd be happy to stay," Reverend McWilliams said.

Nina hesitated. "Are you sure?"

"Of course. Go with God, Nina," he said. Nina was so pleased with his comment about Bunny Pringle that she didn't feel her usual spasm of annoyance.

As she walked down the front hall, she heard him say to Francesca, "Now, what the Bible tells you to do about Friendbook is—"

She was almost tempted to stay and hear the rest of this remarkable sentence, but instead she stepped outside, letting the door swing shut behind her. She began running as soon as she was off the porch, finding her stride quickly, feeling her heart start pumping and the muscles in her legs working. As always, she felt a foolish jolt of pride: she was running, she was a runner, she was one of *them*.

Nina wished she could ask Reverend McWilliams what the Bible told her to do about David. But the problem with that was that Nina knew what the Bible would tell her: have nothing to do with him ever again. It was sound advice, just not the advice that she wanted. She thought perhaps that she could second-guess the Bible. Or not second-guess it—outsmart it. What if she looked for guidance in some other way? What if she looked for a sign? What if, just for argument's sake, she enabled the voice mail on her phone and listened to what David had to say? She could do that when she got home and it wouldn't really *mean* anything.

But Nina didn't have to wait until she got home. When she

crested the slight rise on Blue Heron Bridge, she saw David waiting on the other side. He was far away, but she recognized the clean lines of his body, she knew the way he shook one foot slightly to loosen his ankle, she remembered the fresh-yet-sweaty smell of his red shirt when she had pressed her face against it. These things were as familiar to Nina as the nighttime breathing of her children.

Every pore on her skin opened with pleasure and longing. That is the problem with bodies: they don't think of anything but themselves.

David looked up and raised his hand to her, but only slightly, as though he were afraid she wouldn't acknowledge him. Nina could not wave and run at the same time; she only smiled. So he'd had an affair with a woman even a *minister* thought was an idiot. That was nothing compared to the force of Nina's feelings, nothing that should bother someone like her.

As she ran toward him, Nina felt for a moment that she was leaving a trail behind her, like a comet. But instead of rocks and dust, the trail she was leaving was made of rose petals and sugar and bits of brightly colored paper, and these were being swept off the bridge in the wind, over the water, over the beach, into the city, so that the people out there would get a tiny taste of the sweetness that was Nina's now, of the happiness she knew. Because they would never experience anything like it themselves, Nina thought. Never, never, never.

THAT DANCE YOU DO

....

The cake you bake on the morning of your son's eighth birthday party is strangely slanted to one side. You check the oven rack but it looks perfectly straight. You wonder uneasily if maybe the house is canted on its foundation. Your children could be growing up with one leg longer than the other. Maybe you should call someone to come check out the house, but that is a problem for another day. Right now you need to decide what to do about the cake. You could cut the top off the cake to level it, but it's chocolate with vanilla frosting and a lot of crumbs would show. Best to just frost it as is and hope the slope isn't that noticeable.

The theme of today's party is magic, and you opted for the basic rectangle cake—or trapezium, as the case may be—and you bought a little plastic magician cake decoration, which you stick on the cake right now with a flourish.

Just at this moment, the birthday child runs into the kitchen. He stops when he sees the cake. "Why is the man skiing?" he asks, pointing to the magician figurine.

"Long story," you say. "Happy birthday, darling!"

He hugs you and you lean down and kiss the top of his head.

"Can I have waffles with strawberries as a special birthday breakfast?" he asks.

You would love to make him waffles with strawberries and

sit in the warm morning sunshine of your kitchen and tell him about the day he was born, and how when he turned twenty-four hours old, you cried because you never wanted him to get any bigger.

But just then the doorbell rings with the balloon delivery. You ordered fifty helium-filled balloons but what actually arrives is a helium tank and fifty uninflated balloons.

The stoned-seeming teenager who delivers them assures you that it's really easy to blow the balloons up, and perhaps it might be under other circumstances, but with the help of two small excited children (the doorbell woke your younger son) it is nearly impossible. Eventually, you blow up all the balloons and tie most of them in bunches around the house and yard, and even wrap blue crepe around the oak in front of the house. You do not ask yourself how many of the little boys invited to the party will notice these decorations because you do not want to know the answer. This is merely something you do for children's birthday parties, something that is always done. For you and countless other parents, it is just part of that dance you do.

While your husband mows the lawn and your children are mesmerized by *Charlotte's Web* on the TV, you heat up the iron, put on your iPod, and settle down for a pleasant thirty minutes of making T-shirts for the goody bags.

Earlier, you had designed and printed out eleven T-shirt transfers that say "Thanks for helping us celebrate!" along with an illegally downloaded image of a magician's hat. Yes, you know that T-shirts are unnecessary and a little over-the-top, but it was the one bit of party-planning you actually enjoyed doing.

However, when you iron the first transfer on, you realize that you forgot to reverse the lettering when you printed them and now it's backward on the shirt. "Fuck me," you say, much more loudly than you had intended because of the iPod.

"What happened?" your younger son says in a bored voice. The birthday child doesn't even bother to inquire.

So instead of the relaxing half hour you had envisioned, you have a hectic ninety minutes of reprinting all the T-shirt transfers, rummaging through your children's dressers in hopes of finding a plain white T-shirt, removing a very old spaghetti-sauce stain from said T-shirt, and finally ironing all the transfers on.

When you emerge from the laundry room, hot and sweaty and irritable, you find your husband sitting on the couch, holding the birthday child, who is sad because Charlotte died at the end of the movie. (You own the book but have a bad habit of not completing things and evidently he wasn't prepared for this.)

You sit down on the couch next to them and reach out tentatively to touch your son's back. "I know it's hard," you say. He says nothing and buries his head against your husband's chest.

A rush of tenderness sweeps over you. "I can't believe he was born eight whole years ago," you marvel to your husband.

He looks at you, and then down at the top of your son's head. "Eight long years," he says.

Your children are starting to get cranky from hunger and you haven't been to the store recently except to buy party food, so you and your husband load them in the car and go to McDonald's.

Once there, your husband gives the boys a small lecture on the cost-benefit analysis of ordering a Happy Meal with an inferior toy in it versus saving the price of several Happy Meals and buying a real toy from the toy store. They listen pretty tolerantly (they've heard it before) and then insist on Happy Meals anyway.

Your husband has a salad, and you have black coffee and fold miniature origami birthday hats for the goody bags. The birthday boy saw this on TV and you bought the origami paper and he did exactly two before losing interest. You have read somewhere that origami is supposed to have a soothing effect on the mind but, personally, you find all these little folds just maddening.

Your children are playing with their junky toys and eating their Happy Meals and seem, well, happy. They do keep opening their mouths to show each other chewed-up food, though.

You sigh and say to your husband, "The road to manners is a long one."

"Yes," he agrees, "and possibly you can't get there from here."

Your children finish eating and run off to the play area, leaving behind a mess of crumbs and paper that looks like something you might find under a park bench after a bad storm. You force your husband to fold a paper hat, but either his thumbs are too big or else he's pretending ineptitude to get out of doing any more.

You are about to point out the unfairness of this when there's a wail from the play place. You realize your children are fighting, rolling around on the floor, actually engaged in a *brawl*, though with each other, thankfully. Is it possible to sink any lower than to have children so ill-behaved they stand out even at McDonald's?

You and your husband separate them, saying repeatedly that you don't *care* who started it, and march them out to the car. And so you drive home, the boys not speaking to each other, you still annoyed about the lack of origami help, and your husband tapping out work e-mails on his BlackBerry.

But you must remember: this is an extremely typical preparty family atmosphere, and anyone who tries to tell you otherwise is lying.

Time to fill the goody bags and you realize that you have either miscounted or forgotten someone, but you have eleven guests coming and only ten goody bags. A quick scour of the house reveals that the only other paper bag is one from Victoria's Secret. It is hard to imagine what will be worse, trying to persuade some little boy to accept a pink goody bag when all the other ones are blue, or having to see the parent of the Victoria's Secret bag recipient at school.

You wonder if your children's main memories of you will be your inattention to detail. Like last year when your older son had to take cello lessons at school and you neglected to buy the special cello chair and spike holder, so at the spring recital, he had to go onstage with a ceramic bread bin and a bathmat.

But just then your younger son comes in and sees what you are doing. "Oh, Mommy," he breathes. "Can I have the pretty bag with the stripes? Please?"

"Of course you can," you answer, and he runs off happily.

Maybe they are too young to hold a grudge, or too immature to realize the ramifications of certain actions. Or possibly they have just had limited exposure to mothers who do this kind of thing effortlessly. (You've been pretty careful in your friend selection.) But whatever the reason, right now, for the moment, for a little while longer, you are still okay.

. .

You're on your way to the laundry room to look for the camisole you normally wear under the low-cut shirt you've just put on when the doorbell rings.

You answer and a middle-aged man who looks like a suburban serial killer peers down the front of your shirt and says, "Hello, I'm Manny the Magician."

You experience a moment of profound hindsight, in which you see the wisdom of booking a little more in advance so you don't have to settle for third-rate children's entertainers.

"Hello," you say. "Come on in. You're a bit early."

Manny explains that he's gotten the time of the party wrong but you suspect he's early because he doesn't have anything better to do. He's a mild-mannered, slope-shouldered, balding man wearing bifocals and carrying a tattered duffel bag that presumably holds all his magician supplies. So far he doesn't seem very magical or thrilling, but even worse, when you take his jacket you see that he's wearing a football jersey with the number 16 on it.

Now, it so happens that you've had fifteen sexual partners in your lifetime and seeing Manny the Magician standing there in your front hall labeled number sixteen fills you with an uneasy sense of predestination. Is this where that bright and shining corridor that was your twenties and thirties has led you?

Manny looks at you expectantly. "I need a place to change," he says.

You lead him up to your bedroom—not ideal in that the bed looks like a gypsy's tent made of different-colored lingerie tossed about in your search for the one camisole you still can't find. Also, your diaphragm case is on the nightstand along with a copy of *Alien & Possum: Friends No Matter What*. But you reckon Manny's seen worse and anything to get him out of that shirt.

Still, you are unprepared when he emerges five minutes later in a full-length pale blue gown and peaked hat. He looks like a Ku Klux Klan Grand Wizard. It would be comical if it were not so at odds with Manny's worn face and the bifocals. In a different way, it makes you feel just as awful as the football jersey.

Because you are not insane, and because you do occasionally plan ahead, you have hired a teenage babysitter to help today and she arrives just on time. Her name is Rebecca and she is a redhead and just beautiful with that almost-blue, transparent skin that redheads can have, her hair like a lick of flame.

You and she set up an obstacle course in the backyard, using plastic cones, streamers, and some car tires. A group of trained monkeys could memorize it in less than a minute, but it will probably prove too complicated for a dozen overexcited little boys.

You look at Rebecca as she kneels on the grass, stapling streamers to the ground, and it occurs to you that although you know she is beautiful, possibly Rebecca doesn't know this yet. Also that it's not really a kind of beauty appreciated much by teenagers. You wonder suddenly which table Rebecca sits at during lunch and do the other girls save her a place or does she have to get there quickly, does she have a boyfriend, is he a senior, does he genuinely like her or is he using her for sex, is he out of her league, will he break her heart? You have a sudden longing to be in high school again, where you would know the answers to all these questions, and everyone else would know, too.

· ·

The first guest to arrive is Kenny, a Korean kid, and as soon as the birthday boy sees him, his eyes get very big and he says, "Oh, shit! Kenny's allergic to chocolate and I forgot to tell you, Mommy!"

You suppose you should be upset by the swearing, but it's fairly obvious where he picked up that habit, isn't it? Besides, Kenny's mother speaks barely any English and you're pretty sure she didn't catch that. You are far more concerned about the allergy.

You give Kenny's mom a big reassuring smile and as soon as Kenny is inside with the door shut, you ask, "Is it true about the chocolate cake?"

"Yes," Kenny says.

"How allergic?" you ask. "What happens if you eat it?" If it's just a headache or something, you might be tempted to let him deal with it.

"Hives," Kenny says. "And trouble breathing."

Okay, probably best not to let him deal with it. "Are you allergic to anything else?" you ask.

Truly, it would be simpler to take Kenny into the kitchen and show him the four or five food items you actually have in stock, but he has already run off toward the backyard, his shoes making little squeaks against your floor.

After that, kids start arriving very quickly, dropped off by parents who are presumably excited about having two whole hours to themselves, the lucky bastards.

At one point you answer the door and there is a man you've never seen before and a vaguely creepy teenager. You are about to tell them that they must have the wrong house and that you're really terribly busy, when the man holds out his hand and says, "I'm Caleb's father. Thank you so much for inviting him."

Caleb is the new kid in class and you invited him so he wouldn't feel left out, but you haven't seen him before. Or rather, you had seen him before, but didn't realize who he was. He is nearly as tall as you and seems to have the beginnings of a mustache. He's in second grade? You have your doubts about that, but, more important, you have your doubts about Caleb, who is giving you a slow sinister smile. It may have been a while, a long while, since you were in school, but you still recognize this kid for what he is: a troublemaker.

The last kid is deposited by a harassed mother balancing a fussy child of breast-feeding age on her hip. As soon as the child sees you, she holds out her arms longingly, and glancing down, you realize that you never did locate the camisole that goes under this top. Which means that all the parents so far have had some pretty intense cleavage exposure when you leaned down to welcome their children.

You suppose this will cement your reputation, though what that reputation is, you're not quite sure. Sexy earth mother or disorganized floozy? Really, it is difficult to say. And also way too late, possibly decades too late, to change it now.

The beginning section of the party goes relatively smoothly, or would, if not for Caleb. The first thing he does is come on to Rebecca the babysitter, leering at her and staring her up and down. She gives you a nervous look and you make a sort of helpless gesture, but privately, you are appalled. Realistically, how many times could Caleb have been held back in second grade? Three, at the most?

The children all totally ignore the obstacle course and run around, kicking soccer balls to one another until Caleb boots all the soccer balls over the hedge into the neighbor's yard, where you will have to collect them apologetically tomorrow.

Your husband works in corporate security and you wonder if he could have Caleb's father investigated as a security risk and transferred to some remote location.

The only official party game you have prepared is a store-bought piñata in the shape of a donkey that you hung from a tree. The boys form a line, and you're smart enough to put Caleb last. Then you tie a bandanna around the first child's eyes, give him a broom handle, and let him take a whack at the piñata. And so it goes, with most boys managing to at least hit it, though no one breaks it.

Then Caleb's turn comes and though you tie the bandanna on carefully, he must be able to see slightly because the first thing he does is poke Rebecca in the chest with the broom handle. She gives a little shriek and you quickly spin Caleb by the shoulders until he's facing the right direction. You had known, deep down, that he would be the one to burst the piñata, but you weren't quite prepared for the intensity of his attack. Before you or your husband can react, he has not only broken the donkey open, but pulled it right off the tree and is whacking it to bits.

By the time you wrench the broom handle from his hands, the piñata is lying on the ground like roadkill, and Kenny is so traumatized that he's reverted to the level of a three-year-old and can only stand over the broken piñata, saying, "Donkey okay? Donkey be okay?"

You take Kenny by the hand, scoop up a handful of piñata loot, and walk over and sit with him on the porch. The rest of the children are squabbling over who gets the most candy and toys, but you leave Rebecca and your husband to sort that out. You put your arm around Kenny and distract him by pointing out all the nice candy, a teeny plastic wristwatch and a whistle, and oh, look, a tiny little SpongeBob.

If you were the kind of person who recorded things in notebooks, the first thing you would note under "Birthday Party Improvements" would be "Don't invite Caleb." But you're not that kind of person. In fact, you're the opposite and tend to make the same mistakes over and over. With your luck, your son will decide that Caleb is *soooo cool* and you will be forced to have destructive playdates with him for a long time to come.

It's time for the magic show and you call all the children in and settle them in a group on your living room floor. When Manny enters in all his pale blue splendor, your younger son says "Lady!" in exactly the same fearful whisper as the first time he saw the Easter Bunny at the mall and said, "Mouse!" But everyone else seems pretty unimpressed, and Caleb asks him to move out of the way so they can see the television.

So Manny has to explain that they're not going to watch television, they're going to have a magic show, and he begins. You are not sure you've ever seen a public performer of any variety, even the dog obedience school teacher, with less charisma than Manny. It's depressing, actually, and you wish he were home with his loved ones instead of traipsing about suburbia, humiliating himself.

He does some fairly lame magic tricks, including the jumping paper clips and the four aces. If the children were even a tiny bit older, they would surely be heckling him.

As it is, they are very restless and at one point a small outbreak of poking disrupts things. You nod to Rebecca and she goes and sits in the middle of the group. Caleb smirks at her and moves so his leg is touching hers. She's visibly nervous but the show goes on.

Finally, Manny announces, with no irony whatsoever, that he is also a "balloonologist." He produces a whole bunch of long rubber balloons and says each child can have one and he, Manny, will blow it up and twist it into whatever shape the child requests.

Now, you would think that pretty much any child would have the sense to request something impossible, like a Ferris wheel or a human skeleton. But obviously eight years of TV and computer games have atrophied their brains, and they ask for easy stuff they've seen before, like giraffes and teddy bears. When it's Caleb's turn, you close your eyes and pray silently that he does not request a sex organ or a murder weapon, but all he wants is a dachshund, proving he has even less imagination than everyone else.

With that, the show is over and you release all the kids, who run into the backyard, whacking one another with their balloon animals. Manny begins packing his magic supplies and your husband leads you into the kitchen and asks you two questions: What do you think Manny is wearing under his robe, and where did you find him?

To the first question, you answer, "I don't want to think about it." To the second, you answer, "Liz Beaumont recommended him. She said he was gentle and playful." But now that you think about it, Liz may well have been talking about swimming with the dolphins in the Florida Keys, and the blame for this is yours, and yours alone.

· ·

The rest of the party goes by in a blur, much like your wedding day. In fact, now that you think about it, children's birthday parties are pretty similar to your wedding day: you pay too much attention to meaningless detail, you overinvest in certain decisions, you see your friends but don't really get to interact with them, you end up incredibly stressed, and in retrospect you would certainly do it all much more simply. You don't remember looking at the clock constantly during your wedding reception and thinking, "Thank God, less than an hour till this is over," but quite possibly you did.

You had toyed with the idea of serving Kenny a baked potato with a birthday candle stuck in it, but in the end a search of the basement freezer unearthed a frozen Krispy Kreme doughnut (circa 1980). You defrost that and Kenny seems happy with it, or at any rate, happy enough.

You also have ice cream to serve with the cake, though you bought Neapolitan by mistake, and every single kid wants only one flavor, not all three, so you have to do some careful scooping. Thank God you have Rebecca to scurry back and forth with all the plates and utensils, because your husband is being no help at all.

Annoyingly, he is drinking a scotch on the couch and reading *The Wall Street Journal* as though this party has nothing to do with him. As though you, and a mentally unstable magician, and a redheaded babysitter, and a dozen little boys about to embark on a sugar high, were just some raucous group in a restaurant that he will be careful not to go to again.

After that, the birthday boy opens his presents. You have schooled him to say, "Thank you! I love it!" no matter what the present is, but you haven't quite gotten around to that with his little brother yet. So as each gift is revealed, your younger son is right there to say, "Cool!" or "We already have that!" or "He doesn't like Legos anymore."

But you don't really mind because finally the parents are coming to pick up the guests. Although you do not understand, honestly you do not, how they can be twenty minutes late picking their child up. Is it possible that they don't know how you've been silently beseeching time to speed up for the last two hours? Can they not look back on their own child's party? Have they no compassion, no mercy?

Caleb's father returns to pick Caleb up and you notice some tension in his face when he asks, "How was the party?"

But you know the unwritten rule: unless blood was actually shed, you pretend everything's fine.

"It was great," you say. "I hope Caleb had a good time."

Caleb saunters past you with a self-satisfied smile that makes you want to slap him. You strive for a superior expression, but in reality you probably just look sort of scared and relieved.

After he's gone, the birthday boy leans against you and says, "I don't like him. His breath smells like ketchup and he snapped the heads off all our G.I. Joes."

Ah, your soul mate. You lean down and kiss his neck, even though he squirms away from you. Truly, there is no one like him.

Finally, every last guest is gone, every goody bag taken. Manny has changed back into his street clothes, once again using your bedroom. Weeks later you will discover that a black bra is missing and wonder if he took it, but it is also entirely possible that you left it on the Cub Scout camping trip, given how desperate you were to get back to civilization.

Your husband pays Manny, raising an eyebrow at the price, and then seeing Manny drift back toward the dining room table, he says, "Let us walk you to the door."

You are profoundly grateful to him for this because you suspect Manny is the type who would happily hang around forever, hoping for an invitation to supper. And that would be more than you could bear right now.

But when you all reach the front hall and Manny shrugs into his jacket, he turns to you without outstretched arms and says, "One more thing, I always get a hug before I go."

This is so grim, so unexpected (and yet, really, so hideously predictable), that you are caught entirely flat-footed. Your mind has gone blank with revulsion and you cannot think of a single excuse, so you step forward and let Manny hug you.

It could be worse. Manny doesn't smell bad, or whisper obscenities, or pull a condom magically out of your ear. He does give you a letchy little squeeze, though, which means you will now hate him forever instead of just feel sorry for him. And then it's over.

"Good-bye," Manny says, turning to shake hands with your husband.

"Where's my hug?" your husband asks, and so you laugh when you might have cried.

You and Rebecca pick up all the dirty plates and forks, all the wrapping paper, all the streamers from the obstacle course, trash from a hundred other unidentified sources, and the mutilated piñata. You wonder if perhaps you should take a photograph of it so you can appear on some documentary about career criminals in Caleb's later life. But into the trash bag it goes.

You pay Rebecca and give her a huge tip, even though she looks quite refreshed and happy. She is probably going to go off and make something of the rest of the day while you collapse in a heap. You suddenly long to say, "It is autumn; not without / But within me is the cold." However, you are probably considered eccentric enough without going around quoting Longfellow to teenagers. Instead you say, "Thanks, Rebecca, you saved my life today," and she leaves.

Meanwhile, your husband has fed the children frozen waffles and applesauce, and he pleases you even more by showing you a bottle of chilled champagne and saying that you and he can order a pizza as soon as the boys are asleep.

You would like to put the boys to bed right then and there, but they are filthy and sweaty, streaked with dirt and tears and ice cream. They look like street urchins from some country UNICEF is collecting money for. It doesn't help that one of them is even chewing on a crust of stale bread. You really, really must go to the store.

So you run the bath and they get into it happily, chattering and squirting each other with teeny little water pistols that were part of the piñata booty.

You sit on the floor near the tub with your back against the wall and close your eyes. You hear the sound of water splashing on the floor, but you don't say anything. It's just water, right? It'll dry. Even when one of the children shrieks that he has soap in his eyes, that it stings, it really does, he can't stand it, that he needs a towel right now, you don't move. You just can't.

· ·

But finally, miraculously, your children are in their pajamas, teeth brushed, hair combed, snuggled in their twin beds, with you sitting between them in the rocking chair. All that stands between you and champagne now is the bedtime story.

You start reading a chapter of *The Cricket in Times Square* but after only a page, the birthday boy starts sobbing quietly.

"What's wrong?" you ask, closing the book on your finger.

No answer, just more sobbing.

You glance at your younger child and see that he is so weary he appears to have fallen asleep with his eyes open. You wonder if you will have to shut them for him. But no, he gives a slight jerk, like someone feeling a raindrop, and blink, blink, he's gone.

The birthday child is crying louder now. You sigh. You think of the champagne, the pizza, your husband waiting for you down-stairs. "What's wrong?" you ask again.

"My party's over!" he wails.

Yes, and may the gods delay the next one a hundred years, you think. Aloud you say, "But it was a great party."

"I know, but it's over!"

You sigh again. "Honey, don't cry."

"I can't help it," he says miserably.

"We can't have parties anymore if you're going to cry when they're over," you say. "Do you want me to keep reading?"

He shakes his head against the pillow.

You should put the book away but you are so tired that you just let it fall to the floor and move so you're sitting on the edge of the birthday boy's bed. You hold his hand.

"I was so proud of you today," you say, stroking his arm. "I could tell you were eight years old by the way you thanked your friends for coming to the party and the way you shared your presents with your brother."

Actually, you didn't notice either of these things, but you are too tired to dredge your memory for true examples. These will do. He stops crying and lies quietly, listening. "You are getting so grown up," you say.

You dry his face with your sleeve and then kiss his cheek and whisper good night.

"I'm still sad about the party," he whispers back.

You don't answer. You go out in the hall and turn on the night-light that lights the way to the bathroom. You glance back in and see that he has thrown off the covers, which strikes you as an annoying, melodramatic act, but you let it pass.

"Happy birthday, honey," you say quietly.

You should sit with him until he falls asleep but you really can't stand the thought of further party discussion and anyway, you figure he is too tired to stay awake more than another minute or two. You start down the stairs. You wonder if he realizes that right now, at this instant, you love him more than ever, that you could not love him any more than you do.

DARK MATTER

Here is what Maya's boss said to her after they made love the first time: "Did you know that peanuts are one of the ingredients in dynamite?"

Maya stopped pulling her tights back on and stared at him. He was clearly one of those men whose brains generated arcane semi-educational tidbits of knowledge right after sex. Maya thought of them as come facts.

It was not surprising to learn this about Gildas-Joseph. Maya had always thought that the more intellectual the man, the more liberal he tended to be with come facts. (And she'd slept with enough college professors to know.) She had read somewhere that when very scientific people had near-death experiences, they did not see the light and tunnel like everyone else; they saw the solutions to complex mathematical equations. Come facts were similar, she thought. Something about the brain being swept clean by sexual pleasure and then in the moment of regeneration spawning a fact that the man then rolled over and relayed to the woman.

"Ohhh," Maya said finally. "Interesting."

The way she said the word *interesting* was half-sincere and half-ironic, and so precise were her halves of intonation that nobody hearing her say it could possibly distinguish which she was. It had taken Maya *years* to perfect that tone (all those professors), but now she was able to hit it exactly right every time, the way professional cellists were able to hit the exact center of a musical note. (The sex had been intense; Maya was precariously close to giving her own come fact here.)

She continued to retrieve her clothing from where it was flung around Gildas-Joseph's office. He sat in his desk chair, looking a little dazed.

Although Maya had had a crush on Gildas-Joseph ever since she started working at the library, it was not until tonight when, ironically, the office had celebrated her engagement to Rhodes that anything had happened between them. After work, the entire staff had drunk champagne in the conference room to toast Maya's engagement (it was that kind of office, they celebrated everything, kept a case of discount champagne in the storeroom) and little by little, everyone else had drifted home except for Maya, because Rhodes was working late, and Gildas-Joseph, who told her he wasn't in a hurry because his wife had a harp recital.

So they had taken the rest of the last bottle into Gildas-Joseph's office and he had congratulated her again and then said, "You don't have a ring yet, though."

"Oh, I'm not going to have one," Maya said. "I don't approve of them."

He looked amused. "What's not to approve?"

Maya thought for a minute. "I guess it seems like a place-holder. You know, the man puts the ring on the girl's finger and then—presto!—she's engaged, committed, but *he's* not until the wedding ceremony."

"Some men don't even wear rings then," Gildas-Joseph said.

"And I really hate it when men give girls engagement rings for

Christmas," Maya continued. "Like getting married is a gift, like the man is saying, *If you want it so much, then here, Merry Christmas.*"

He laughed. "You would make a good Frenchman, Maya."

"Is that a compliment?" she asked.

He nodded, looking at her. "I have to say——" he said and hesitated.

"What?" Maya asked. "What were you going to say?"

"That it makes me sad, in a way, to see you get engaged."

(It was the champagne. They never talked like this; honest, they never did. Previously, the most intimate thing Maya had ever said to Gildas-Joseph was that she'd never finished *Great Expectations.*)

"Why?" she asked.

"You know why," he said.

And she did know, of course. She'd only wanted to hear him say it. Maya's knowledge is what led to her clothes being taken off and tossed around and the subsequent come fact. That was a strange thing about getting engaged, something that Maya had not predicted and could not really understand: it made her feel unbelievably sexy, and (as it turned out) not just toward Rhodes.

Maya was relieved when she got home and saw that all the lights were out except the one over the kitchen sink. Rhodes had gone to bed. She parked her car in the driveway and went in through the back door. She turned out the kitchen light and continued quietly along the hall toward their bedroom.

But Rhodes was not asleep. He was in Maya's study, sitting at her computer, wearing nothing but pajama bottoms even though it was January, and updating her antivirus software.

"Hey," he said. "You're late."

"I was finishing the print collection for the Grove Dictionary with Gildas-Joseph," Maya said.

"Zut alors!" Rhodes said promptly.

It was involuntary, Maya thought, like a tic. Whenever she said Gildas-Joseph's name, Rhodes said something in a French accent. She had even learned to compensate for it, to pause briefly, so Rhodes wouldn't miss the rest of what she was saying. It was the same when she mentioned her Australian friend Sophie and he would say a line from *Crocodile Dundee,* or when she talked about her Irish friend Ellen and he would say "Begorrah!" (Luckily, that was pretty much it for Maya's foreign friends.)

"I thought you'd gone to bed," Maya said softly, coming in to stand next to him.

"I'm about to," Rhodes answered. He pushed back the black leather computer chair and pulled her into his lap.

Maya pressed her lips against the bare skin of his shoulder.

Something on the computer screen caught Rhodes's attention and he reached past her to tap a few keys. He put his arm around her waist absently and pulled her closer so she would not fall off his lap.

Maya closed her eyes. Something had happened to time. It did not seem to her that this moment passed so much as she traveled through it, slowly, involuntarily, like standing on the moving walkway at the airport. And Maya vowed that if she got through this moment, if she emerged on the other side, she would never do what she had done tonight again. She meant it. She would never do that again.

· ·

Maya went into Gildas-Joseph's office the next morning to tell him that she couldn't see him anymore and then they had sex on his desk. (This was something Maya had noticed about herself, a sort of inner contrariness; she drank the most on nights she went to the bar vowing to have only club soda.)

Afterward, Gildas-Joseph said, "*Almost* is the longest word in the English language with all the letters in alphabetical order."

Really, what had Maya expected, getting involved with a librarian?

"And *rhythm* is the longest English word without—" Gildas-Joseph continued, but Maya put her finger against his lips.

"One's your limit," she said.

Gildas-Joseph looked startled. Of course, he didn't know Maya was talking about come facts—he was most likely unaware the term even existed—and probably thought she was talking about sex. Maybe he thought she meant this was the only time they would ever do it (though this time, in fact, made it twice), or maybe he thought she was remarking that he could do it once. Maya did not enlighten him.

"Until later then," he said.

(A door in her mind opened and Rhodes said quickly, "*A tout à l'heure!*" and then Maya slammed the door shut.)

"Until later," she agreed.

In the weeks and months that followed Maya sometimes felt like she was watching her life happen to someone else: Look at the nice pretty girl get up every morning and run five miles. Watch her come home and bring her fiancé a cup of tea before he even wakes up. See her get in bed and make love to him sometimes, still sweaty from her run. ("Do you know that dark matter seems to *comprehend* how the visible matter is distributed?" her fiancé tells her afterward. "Did you know Diet Coke would be green if they didn't add food coloring?")

Watch her go to her job as a librarian, and do in a few hours the work that used to take her all day. She has to be efficient, because any moment, her boss might have a break in his schedule and then they can be together, they can look at each other in the lounge, they can hold hands in the microfiche room, they can make love in her boss's car, where the leather seats leave strange patterns on the girl's skin.

The days the girl works at home are even nicer and after she showers, she puts on her kimono and works on her computer until lunchtime, when her boss drives over from the library and parks his car around the block. He knocks on the back door, and they make love on the kitchen table, or on the living room floor, because they cannot wait to get back to the bed in the girl's guest room, though they do eventually get there and make love again, more slowly, and thoroughly, so thoroughly; there is nothing they wouldn't do for each other. "God, you are fantastic," the girl's boss says. And then he tells her that humans share 60 percent of their DNA with fruit flies.

Fruit flies are a problem at the girl's house, which gets messier and messier. She has thrown away the fruit that was rotting in the bowl, but the fruit flies persist. The fruit bowl remains empty, as does the pantry and the refrigerator. She never has time to go to the store—"Why is it we are always eating Indian takeout?" asks the girl's fiancé in an Indian accent—to call her parents, to go to the dentist, or to put away laundry.

Sometimes the girl wonders why she wants her boss when

she already has a fiancé, and she can't really explain it, even to herself, other than that she has always wanted her boss, always loved the traces of silver in the hair near his temples, and his dark eyes, and his faint French accent. And now she has him, and she can't get over it, she feels a little shiver of delight whenever she thinks about it, the way she can't get over it when she buys something very expensive, like a Chanel handbag, that she keeps taking out of the wrapping and looking at and marveling at how it's now hers and how this beautiful object takes on the shine of familiarity. She used to look at it in the store and wish she owned it and now she does. Probably her boss would not like to be compared to a handbag, even a French one, and the girl doesn't see him as an object, but the thrill of ownership persists.

It seems to the girl that she's aware now of an undercurrent of sex in the world, that she has slipped down into it. The world seems to be awash with sex in a way it wasn't before. It's everywhere—books, movies, commercials—and in real life, too. Men look at the girl in a new way. She doesn't want anything to do with these other men, she is happy with the two she has, but she likes the attention, she is amused by the way they are suddenly everywhere: in the street, at the library, at the park, at the liquor store.

"Did you know the pressure in a champagne bottle is the same as the pressure in a double-decker bus tire?" the guy at the liquor store tells Maya.

Because, of course, the world is suddenly full of come facts, too.

· ·

Maya got to Rhodes's parents' house late for dinner. She hung her coat in the closet and headed to the kitchen. "Sorry I'm late," she said in the doorway. "I was having drinks with my friend Vanessa."

"Blimey," said Rhodes, startling Maya until she remembered that Vanessa (whom she hadn't actually seen in months) was British. Rhodes was sitting with Magellan at the kitchen table and had a textbook open in front of him. Desmond was across from them with the newspaper.

"That's all right, dear," Hazelene said from where she was standing by the stove. "I just finished setting the table in the dining room. Would you like a drink?"

"I'll help myself," Maya said. She got a wineglass from the cupboard and filled it from a bottle of red that sat on the table near Rhodes.

"Hey," he said, reaching for her hand. "How are you? How's Vanessa?"

"Good and good," Maya said, kissing him. "Hey, Magellan. What are you studying?"

"Hi," Magellan said, her usual lackluster greeting. "Rhodes is prepping me for the geography bee tomorrow."

"Can I help with dinner?" Maya asked Hazelene. She always had to remind herself to do this, because being at Rhodes's parents' house felt so much like being a teenager that she automatically sank into teenage lassitude. So did Rhodes, she'd noticed, and so did Magellan (who actually was a teenager), and Desmond had apparently not done anything to help around the house for thirty years, so it was very easy to let Hazelene take care of everything.

"Oh, no, dinner's almost ready," Hazelene said. "You just keep us all company."

So Maya pulled out a chair at the kitchen table and sat next to Desmond.

He looked up from the paper. "Did you know that right-handed people live, on average, nine years longer than left-handed people?"

(Had he just come? Maya didn't want to think about that very much, but it did seem like an obvious conclusion.)

"Interesting," she said. "Did you know that there's a high tendency in twins for one to be left-handed?"

Desmond frowned. "Is that true?"

Now, how sexist was that? Here Maya had spent half a lifetime listening to men tell her come facts and having to act fascinated, and the one and only time she tells a man one, he questions its veracity!

"Yes, it's true," she said. "I designed the website for the Southpaws Club of Illinois once."

"Mmmm," Desmond said, obviously not impressed.

Now Maya wondered if it actually was true, that thing about twins. But they paid her to design, not fact-check.

Across the table, Rhodes read to Magellan from the textbook. "Which Canadian province produces more than half of the country's manufactured goods?"

"No idea," Magellan said. "I can't name any Canadian provinces."

"I'll give you a hint," Rhodes said. "It has access to the Saint Lawrence Seaway."

"I just *said* I don't know any provinces."

"It's the second largest one." Rhodes used the tone of someone being overly generous.

"Either do sounds-like or go on to the next question," Magellan said.

"Dinner's ready," Hazelene said then, and they all moved into the dining room, although Rhodes brought the book along and asked questions to them as a group. They ate tacos (Hazelene even cooked things that teenagers like) and talked about geography and Magellan left the table three separate times to answer the phone.

"Our lives are dictated by modern technology," Desmond said to Maya, after the third time.

Maya wasn't so sure about that. The phone that Magellan kept getting up to answer seemed to be a relic from the early 1970s that had been bolted to the kitchen wall ever since Maya had started dating Rhodes seven years ago and probably for a few decades before that. Although Magellan stretched the curly yellow cord connected to the receiver as far as possible, they could still hear her saying, "I'm sure I'll be eliminated in the first round."

"No kidding," Rhodes said. "She couldn't even name the highest mountain in Europe."

"Mont Blanc." Maya spoke before she thought. Gildas-Joseph had a summer house in Haute-Savoie.

"*Ah, la vache,*" Rhodes said, looking surprised. "Very good, Maya."

After dinner, Maya helped Hazelene clear the table and wash the dishes. "Thank you, dear," Hazelene said. "It was good to see you tonight. Rhodes says you've been working so hard lately."

Maya felt a tiny flicker of alarm. How hard could you have to work, realistically, as a part-time librarian and website designer? And the fact that Rhodes had noticed this, had thought it worthy of discussing with Hazelene, troubled her.

"Yes," she said slowly. "But it won't last forever."

Because it wouldn't, she and Gildas-Joseph knew that. It

would be over. Any day now, Maya promised herself. Or at least soon.

"How was your day, Hazelene?" she asked, glad she'd remembered, because that was another thing that tended to happen at Rhodes's parents' house, you forgot that his parents were actual people with lives.

"Oh, it was very boring," Hazelene said. "I waited all morning for the dryer repairman and he finally showed up and the dryer began working perfectly! So he says, 'Don't you know how to turn it *on*?' And I snap, 'Of course I do, I'm not a moron!' And then we have ten minutes of very tense silence, waiting for the dryer to stop working, which it eventually did. But not before I began thinking, Darn, *could* I be a moron? Would I know if I were?"

Maya laughed. Hazelene did not deal in come facts, or even geographical ones. She told stories. Even if the world were ending, even if they were fleeing Rome as it burned, Hazelene would be jogging beside her, panting out an anecdote about the cashier at the supermarket. Maya loved that about her.

Emily from the library was pregnant and having a cocktail party, because, she said, as soon as the baby was born that spring, she expected their social life to grind to a halt and she wanted to get in as much entertaining as possible before that. Emily herself was drinking a "mocktail" but she directed Maya and Rhodes to her dining table, which was set up as a bar, complete with a pimply-faced high school bartender.

Maya asked for a glass of red wine and Rhodes asked for a beer and then they turned right around and there were Gildas-Joseph and his wife, Adèle.

Maya had known, of course, that they would be here. She and Gildas-Joseph had discussed it and agreed to attend, agreed there was no reason not to, that they could handle it. They had also agreed not to have sex that day, but now Maya found herself wishing that they had. It might have relaxed her.

"Maya, hello," said Adèle. "It seems like forever since we've seen you."

Maya smiled and said hello and introduced Rhodes. She had met Adèle at countless other office parties, but she had not paid attention to her the way she did now. Gildas-Joseph seldom talked about Adèle, but he had told Maya once that she and Adèle were opposites in every way. Maya could deduce a lot of things from that statement without meeting Adèle, like that Maya was interested in sex and Adèle wasn't, and Maya paid a lot of attention to Gildas-Joseph and Adèle didn't, and Maya was very ironic and Adèle was very serious. But it was different to see Adèle in person.

So, Maya thought, her eyes flickering over Adèle, this was her opposite. Adèle was taller than Maya, but nearly everyone was taller than Maya. Adèle had close-cropped black hair, almond-shaped gray eyes, and a long graceful neck. Maya had long brown hair that hung halfway down her back in a wavy tangle, and big brown eyes, and her neck was okay, but not swanlike. Adèle was pretty, but this did not bother Maya because Maya had always known she herself was closer to *sexy* on the pretty-sexy spectrum. Adèle's outfit was less an outfit than a number of very gauzy overlapping layers in jewel tones. (Maya would have bet that it was not possible to put on all those layers in the same order twice.) The gauzy layers looked lovely on Adèle's tall thin body; Maya would have looked like someone who got dressed while running out of a burning building. But that was okay, too, because Maya liked her own clothes, her brown velvet jeans and cream-colored sweater. Adèle was also sophisticated, you couldn't get around that, and although the opposite of sophisticated was *unsophisticated,* Maya preferred to think Gildas-Joseph considered her natural and uncomplicated. Adèle had a regal, remote, delicately reserved demeanor. Maya didn't know exactly what her own demeanor was but suspected it was more along the lines of a golden retriever running into the house after a long walk. And that was okay because Maya liked dogs. (She happened to know Adèle did not.)

Apparently Rhodes had never met Adèle before, or spoken to her at length, because now he said, "What do you do, Adèle?"

"I teach the harp," Adèle said. Her French accent was stronger than her husband's.

"Teach it to do what?" Rhodes asked. (In her heart, Maya had known he would say that.)

But she had forgotten this about Rhodes: some people made stupid jokes and looked pleased with themselves, but Rhodes made stupid jokes and then looked sheepish, which made the other person laugh.

Adèle laughed.

"Now, is it true that harpists use only the first four fingers?" Rhodes said.

Which sounded like a come fact but it wasn't; that was the way Rhodes talked. He knew a little bit about *everything.* Once when he had taken Maya to a family reunion, the whole extended family—twenty-two relatives plus Maya—had played Trivial Pursuit against Rhodes, and Rhodes still won. (Maya had not known a single answer, and might as well have stayed in the kitchen and made potato salad.)

"Yes, that is true," Adèle said. "The little finger cannot pluck the strings with sufficient force."

Rhodes looked thoughtful. "Don't people ever try to build their little fingers up? Wouldn't that give you a professional edge?"

So he and Adèle had a long conversation about pinkies and orchestras and classical music and handgrips and even detoured briefly into the history of the harp while Maya drank red wine with a hand that trembled (perhaps she should do hand exercises like Adèle) and tried to think of nonincriminating things to say to Gildas-Joseph.

She was so flustered she could barely meet Gildas-Joseph's eyes, but when she did, he smiled at her reassuringly. She should have known he would be able to handle such a situation. He was sophisticated, just like his wife.

"How is the jazz section of Grove going?" he asked, and Maya gratefully launched into a description so detailed and boring that if anyone listening *had* known they were having an affair, they probably would have thought she was trying to get Gildas-Joseph to break up with her.

Then there was one of those little shifts that happen at parties and suddenly Gildas-Joseph was talking to Rhodes, and Maya was talking to Adèle.

"Remind me of the names of your children again," Maya said, not because she needed reminding but because she was afraid she hadn't known them before and knew them now.

"Mary Ellen, Lorraine, and George," Adèle said, smiling, and Maya marveled again at how names that were so boring in English could sound so pretty in French.

"And how old are they?" Maya asked, though of course she knew that, too: fifteen, twelve, and nine.

Adèle answered and then smiled again and said, "I think I

remember Gildas-Joseph telling me you and Rhodes were engaged?"

"Yes, we are," Maya said.

"Congratulations," Adèle said. "Are you planning the wedding, or happy just to be engaged for the moment?"

"I think just happy to be engaged," Maya said. "Weddings can be such a nightmare."

"I agree," Adèle said. "So much pressure on the brides these days!" Her voice was soft and well-modulated even when she was exclaiming.

"Well, yes," Maya said. "And I don't even like to plan a trip to the corner store."

"Exactly," Adèle said.

What a tedious conversation, Maya thought. Is this what Gildas-Joseph's whole life was like? Were conversations like these what he wanted?

In the car on the way home, she said to Rhodes, "Do you think Adèle is my opposite?"

"Your opposite?" Rhodes frowned. "In what way?"

"Every way," Maya said.

"I think your true opposite would be some elderly Polynesian man in a fishing boat off the coast of Perth," Rhodes said. (Maya checked on the Internet later and found that the coast of Perth was directly on the other side of the planet.)

"Well, maybe," Maya said. "But what I mean is, I guess, is she better than me in some way? Prettier or smarter or more sophisticated?"

"Prettier?" Rhodes said, sounding mystified. "Smarter? You're the smartest person I know, Maya."

That certainly wasn't true, but Maya knew that on some very

important level, he believed it. And that was what was so wonderful about Rhodes.

One week in late February, Rhodes and Gildas-Joseph told Maya
the *same* come fact, that there was a movement to reinstate Pluto's
status as a planet. When Maya was much younger, two different
dates in one weekend had taken her to the same restaurant, and
Maya felt now what she'd felt then. Namely, that standards were
slipping.

She assumed the business about Pluto had been on the news
(otherwise it was a coincidence of nearly unbelievable propor-
tions) just as years ago she'd assumed the restaurant had recently
been favorably reviewed somewhere.

"Do you think I don't read the paper or watch the news?" she
said to Rhodes, who gave her the come fact second.

"You don't," Rhodes said.

That was true (she didn't have time anymore, for one thing),
but Maya thought it was beside the point.

What was she doing with a fiancé *and* a lover if they were
so similar that at the moment of complete sexual oblivion (or
ten seconds after), they had the same thought? This caused Maya
some discomfort, because actually Rhodes and Gildas-Joseph
were similar on a lot of levels, sometimes they even made the
same joke, and they both liked to talk about dark matter.

But in the end, Maya came to pretty much the same conclusion as the one she'd reached years earlier: Better to have dinner
at the uninspired choice of restaurant than have no date at all.
Better to be told an uninspired come fact than spend that half
hour cleaning out the refrigerator (something Maya hadn't done
for weeks). Better to settle for a substandard come fact than to

have that come fact given to some other girl. Because Maya could not have borne it if either Rhodes or Gildas-Joseph made love to some other girl.

And yes, she knew that was a double standard.

Gildas-Joseph went away for three days over Easter and Maya had expected to miss him unbearably. She thought she would fill the time by doing all the things she'd neglected. She would clean the whole house, dust the blades of the ceiling fans, vacuum the refrigerator coils, maybe hire a chimney sweep.

But she didn't do any of those things. She spent all the time with Rhodes. She brought him lunch in his office, they went to the movies in the middle of the afternoon, they took a shower together, and they went to a stationery store to look at wedding invitations, but were too intimidated by the questions the saleswoman asked to order anything. Instead they came home and made love three times in a row and ordered Chinese food and drank beer in bed and Rhodes told her that the name Google is a play on the word *googol,* which refers to the number one followed by one hundred zeroes. Then he did an impersonation of himself telling that to the Chinese-food delivery girl after sex (not that he'd *had* sex with the Chinese-food delivery girl, it was a sort of imaginary impersonation) and her saying later to her friends, "Oh, he very smart, he tell me a lot about search engines." Because Rhodes knew about come facts, Maya had told him long ago.

Maya began getting dressed. "Do you think I'm sober enough to drive?" she asked.

"Sure, it was only half a beer," Rhodes said, from the bed. "Where are you going?"

"I have to pick up some dry cleaning, and maybe go into work for a while," Maya said, but actually she wanted to surprise Gildas-Joseph and pick him up at the airport. She couldn't wait to see him.

One Sunday they went over to Rhodes's parents for brunch and ate eggs Benedict and then they all sat around the living room, reading the paper.

Hazelene was doing the crossword. "What's a nine-letter French word meaning 'full and direct state control of a country's economy and social institutions'?"

"Dirigisme," Maya said.

"Ohhh, thank you," Hazelene said happily, scratching away with her pencil.

Maya set aside the Arts section. "My boss told me that," she said. "Gildas-Joseph."

"*C'est la fin des haricots,*" Rhodes said.

Obviously Maya did not have to quote a source. Rhodes's family (except for Magellan) knew all sorts of stuff like that. They probably would have been *more* suspicious if she hadn't known the answer. Maya brought Gildas-Joseph into the conversation for only one reason: the pleasure of saying his name aloud. Even if it was to her future mother-in-law.

Maya and Rhodes went to the movies one Friday night and as they were waiting in line, Rhodes looked over her shoulder and said softly, *"Poser un lapin,"* and so Maya knew even before she turned that Gildas-Joseph must be there.

He was, just coming in the doors with Adèle. How strange that Maya had never run into him anywhere outside of work for three years and now she saw him here.

"Maya, Rhodes, hello again," Adèle exclaimed softly. "So delightful to see you."

They were right behind Maya and Rhodes in line and the line was moving slowly, so they had to have a long four-way chat about the weather and Henry VIII (they were going to see *The Other Boleyn Girl*) and how historical movies always seem to get Oscar nominations and the profit margin on movie-theater popcorn and how amazing it was that five hours ago, Maya had been kneeling in front of Gildas-Joseph in the guest bedroom and making him come so powerfully that he could barely manage to tell her afterward how many gallons of water were in the Gulf of Mexico. (They didn't really discuss that last part, but Maya felt it hammering around in her brain, desperate to get out.)

Then, thankfully, Maya and Rhodes bought their tickets and said good-bye and went on into the theater.

"I can't believe we saw them here," Rhodes said. "I didn't think they went to the movies."

"Why not?" Maya said irritably. "Why shouldn't they go to the movies like everyone else?"

"No reason," he said. "I guess I thought they stayed home and listened to chamber music, or maybe only went to movies with subtitles."

Maya had sort of thought this, too. "I know."

"I'm glad they weren't here last week when we came to see *Cloverfield,*" Rhodes said. "I'd feel so inferior."

"Me, too," Maya said.

And then suddenly Adèle was standing next to them, holding out Maya's gloves. "You left these at the ticket window," she said.

"Oh, thank you," Maya said. "I'm always losing them. I've lost count of the places I've left them."

"It might be easier to count the places you *haven't* left them," Rhodes said.

Adèle handed her the gloves and Maya's fingers touched Adèle's briefly. It was a strange sensation.

"Thank you," Maya said.

Adèle smiled. "My pleasure." She walked back up the aisle to where Gildas-Joseph was saving her a seat.

Had Gildas-Joseph seen the gloves at the ticket window? Had he known they were Maya's the same way he would recognize Maya's voice or scent? Had he been looking at them, thinking of her, when his wife innocently picked them up?

Because Adèle *was* innocent, Maya had no doubt of that. Her eyes when she looked at Maya were friendly and interested and utterly without suspicion. Maya felt so sorry for her. Poor Adèle, who knew nothing. Poor Adèle, who did not realize that every day when her husband left for work, he was leaving for Maya's arms, who did not know that Maya had been in Adèle's own home, had made love to Adèle's husband on the foldout couch in the study, and on the floor next to the couch when Maya could no longer stand the pressure of the sofa bed's hard iron bar across her shoulder blades. Adèle did not know that Gildas-Joseph spoke to Maya on his cell phone during George's soccer games, that he called Maya from outside Lorraine's art classes, that Maya was the first person he told when he found cigarettes in Mary Ellen's purse. Adèle knew none of these things. She did not realize that her husband betrayed her ten thousand times in the course of a single day.

The lights went down in the theater and Rhodes reached for Maya's hand. He liked to hold hands at the movies.

But suddenly Maya's hands were icy and she could hardly breathe. She stared at Rhodes in the semi-darkness. She had not thought of this before, not because she hadn't wanted to think of it, not because she was in denial, but because it truly hadn't occurred to her. But it occurred to her now, powerfully: she was betraying Rhodes ten thousand times a day, too.

Maya was meeting Gildas-Joseph at the coffee shop near the university because he had a late meeting and she had just gone to the convenience store for milk and bread and, with any luck, they would have time for a quick coffee and maybe make love in the backseat of Maya's car. This was the way Maya's whole life operated now, insane timings dependent on a little luck, and for the first time in her life, Maya understood that expression about making your own luck because she and Gildas-Joseph did seem to make their own luck, create their own time, when previously no time had existed.

But tonight as she pushed open the glass door of the coffee shop, a voice behind her said, "Hi, Maya."

It was Magellan.

"Hey," Maya said. "What are you doing here?" She was safe in the knowledge that Magellan would never ask what Maya was doing here, because Magellan never talked about anything but herself.

"I'm supposed to meet Angie," Magellan said. Oh, yes, Angie, Magellan's best friend. They giggled behind their hands a lot. It drove Maya crazy.

They were inside the coffee shop now and Maya glanced around. She didn't see Gildas-Joseph or Angie. "Where are you meeting Angie?" she asked.

"I was *supposed* to meet her," Magellan said. "But she just sent me a text."

Sometimes Maya thought that Magellan had been born without a sense of narrative, the way some people were born colorblind. "What did the text say?" she asked.

"Oh, well," Magellan said, "just that she couldn't make it because she was stuck at school."

"Is she not coming at all?" Maya said.

Magellan shook her head.

"Well, come have coffee with me," Maya said. She was wondering how she would be able to get rid of Magellan, who seemed young and defenseless suddenly, more like thirteen than sixteen. How was she planning to get home? It was already dark out.

They went up to the counter and Maya ordered a latte and Magellan ordered a hot chocolate. Maya paid for both. Magellan didn't offer to pay, or say thank you, which Maya knew was because she viewed Maya as a grown-up, like her parents and Rhodes, someone who would automatically take care of her.

They sat together at a table and Magellan said, "You shouldn't ask for a latte, you know."

"Why not?"

"Because *latte* is slang for 'erection' in German."

Now Magellan was telling her come facts! Come facts about coming, even, or at least about sex.

"Really?" said Maya. "How do you know that?"

"Angie told me."

"And how does Angie know?" This is what conversations with Magellan were like, endless question-and-answer sessions that never really went anywhere. Even Socrates would have wanted to strangle her.

"Her grandma told her."

"What kind of grandmother knows that?" Maya asked. "And does it matter if we're not in Germany?"

"Well," Magellan said slowly. "What if the person behind the counter is German and you don't know it?"

This was, believe it or not, actually *the* most interesting thing Magellan had ever said to Maya, and Maya was so caught up in thinking about it that she didn't notice Gildas-Joseph standing by their table.

"Oh, hey, hello," she said, flustered. "Magellan, this is my boss, Gildas-Joseph. And this is Rhodes's sister, Magellan."

"Hi," Magellan said. (Someday Maya was going to have to teach Magellan a more interesting, upbeat way of greeting people.)

"Hello, Magellan," Gildas-Joseph said easily. "Do you mind if I join you ladies?"

"Of course not," Maya said.

He sat down and they smiled at each other across Magellan.

"Magellan is an interesting name," Gildas-Joseph said. "Do you like it?"

Usually people who met Magellan said, *Like the explorer, right?* as though they wanted to quickly establish some rudimentary history knowledge. No one else had ever asked her how she liked being named Magellan in Maya's presence.

"I don't like it," Magellan said. "You can't even tell from looking at it whether it's a boy's or girl's name."

"What would you like your name to be?" he asked.

"Jenny," Magellan said without hesitating. "Or maybe Lynn. Nothing unusual."

"You will probably give your children very ordinary names," Gildas-Joseph said. "And they will give their children unusual names, and it will go on like that for generations."

"Do you think?" Magellan said. Maya could tell Magellan was pleased, maybe because he seemed to take it for granted that she would get married someday. Maya felt a little proprietary thrill. This was *her* lover, charming Magellan, the uncharmable.

"So where are you two going from here?" Gildas-Joseph asked.

"I'm going to the bookstore and then home, I guess," Magellan said.

"How are you getting home?" Maya asked.

"The bus."

"Don't be silly, I'll drive you," Maya said, trying to keep the impatience from her voice. She would have to drive Magellan, there was no way around it.

"Okay," Magellan said agreeably. "Do you care if I go to the bookstore first?"

"No, of course not," Maya said. "I'll wait right here."

Magellan left, leaving her scarf behind on her chair. Maya felt like it was left to keep an eye on them somehow.

"I'm sorry," she said to Gildas-Joseph.

He reached for her hand. "Me, too."

"Did you know *latte* is the German word for 'erection'?"

"The French word is *trique*." He smiled ruefully. "I have one."

Maya looked at him, a look that would have to take the place of a kiss. "I'm sorry," she said again.

"It's okay," Gildas-Joseph said. "You are so good with her, with Magellan."

And then Maya kissed him, coffee shop or no.

Because although she cared enough not to let Magellan take the bus home alone in the dark and possibly be abducted and murdered, and although she once spontaneously bought a silver wishbone charm for Magellan's charm bracelet from the resale shop (it was only a dollar or she wouldn't have bought it), and although sometimes she rode in the backseat and let Magellan ride in the front seat because Magellan tended to get carsick, Maya was not, by any standards you could *ever* apply, good with Magellan.

And that was how Maya knew what she and Gildas-Joseph had, by mutual agreement, promised never to say. He loved her. He really must.

Maya and Gildas-Joseph made love silently, due to the fact that the other people who worked in the library were having a baby shower for Emily in the conference room, which shared a wall with Gildas-Joseph's office. Maya's back was up against the door because they didn't entirely trust the lock, and Gildas-Joseph had his hand over her mouth (he said she was very noisy). They moved slowly, slowly, almost didn't move at all because they were afraid to make the door rattle in its frame.

When they were done, Maya kissed him quietly and, still without speaking, left his office and tiptoed the opposite way of the conference room and out to the parking lot.

She had to stop to put gas in the car on the way home because the tank was nearly empty. Just like the electric bill was overdue and she hadn't returned their DVDs and she and Rhodes took showers by candlelight because something was wrong with the bathroom light fixture and Maya hadn't called an electrician. Maya had more pressing things on her mind these days.

She was standing in the faintly chilly May air, holding the nozzle in the gas tank and shivering slightly, when a bearded man poked his head around the gas pump behind her and said, "Would you like to see something interesting?"

Good God, he was going to expose himself! Maya gasped, which the bearded man apparently took for acquiescence because he walked around the pump (he was fully clothed, thankfully) and stood next to her.

"Look," he said, pointing at the sky. "See that star, the one that's brighter than the others and doesn't twinkle?"

"Venus," Maya said. (Hey, she didn't live with Rhodes for nothing.)

"Yes!" the bearded man said in a slightly challenging tone. "But did you know that Venus is visible at both dusk and dawn today and tomorrow? And that happens only once every eight years."

"Oh," Maya said. "Interesting."

"Isn't it?" the man said, and he looked like he had more to say, but Maya had finished filling her car and she trilled her fingers at him and got back inside.

As she drove away, she wondered why the man had singled her out for his impromptu science lecture. Did she look too passive, too beaten down? Would someone more assertive have whacked him with her purse and told him to keep his come facts to himself?

Because, she realized, he *had* told her a come fact. A stranger had told her a come fact. Maybe it was like a law of physics, she thought suddenly, and even though the man who had made her come hadn't told her a come fact, the very next man she saw did. Maybe it was some natural set of checks and balances, and for a few minutes there, the cosmos had been out of kilter. It pleased her to think that she had triggered a universal imbalance (how many people could say that?) and then she was suddenly pierced with melancholy. She wanted to tell someone about this, but the person she wanted to tell was Rhodes.

Gildas-Joseph lay back against the pillows on the bed in Maya and Rhodes's guest room. He pushed Maya's hair back from her face gently with his thumb and said, "Did you know the name Vermont comes from *verts monts,* French for 'green mountains'?"

"Yes, actually I did know that," Maya said. (She'd read a book called *Smart About the Fifty States* over and over on car trips as a child.) She smiled. "Does it count as a come fact if I already knew it?"

Gildas-Joseph knew about come facts now; Maya's betrayal of Rhodes was complete.

Gildas-Joseph hesitated. "Maybe not. But there was a reason I told you that."

"Then it definitely doesn't count," Maya said. She was distracted by looking at him. Even after all this time, she could not get over the fact that he was here, with her. "It counts only if it pops into your head sort of involuntarily." Then she looked at him. "What was the reason?"

He turned on his side. "Because I've been offered a job there," he said. "A tenure track position at the University of Vermont."

"I don't want you to go," Maya said instantly. She said it as instinctively as she would have held on to her purse if someone tried to snatch it. *You can't have that, it's mine, it belongs to me.*

"It's a good offer, Maya."

They were silent for a moment.

She swallowed. "You've already accepted, haven't you?"

"Maya—" he began and then stopped. "Yes. I leave in a month."

She turned away from him and stared at the wall. But she did not resist when he moved closer and put his arms around her. He rested his hand on her stomach and she reached down and held it.

"I wanted to tell you before," he said.

She sighed. "It's okay."

She thought that soon she would once again have time to grocery shop, she could even go to the farmers' market, she could make summer gazpacho from the freshest, ripest tomatoes and garnish it with avocado slices. She wished the idea did not make her so unbearably sad.

Maya was preoccupied by dark matter in the month that followed. This was evidently the person she'd become, someone who was mindlessly unfaithful and went around thinking about dark matter.

Of course Gildas-Joseph would go to Vermont with his family. They had always said that they could not continue seeing each other forever. Maya had never thought about leaving Rhodes for Gildas-Joseph, not for one single second. How could she be a stepmother to three children whose names she couldn't even pronounce properly in French? (Mary Ellen was particularly hard to say.) And although in the past Maya had thought about leaving Rhodes, sometimes seriously, she could never do it. Rhodes made life interesting. It was really as simple as that. And because he was interested in her, Maya became interesting, too. Without him, she had a feeling she would be nothing in Gildas-Joseph's eyes.

So instead Maya thought about dark matter.

"Is it true," she said to Rhodes, "that dark matter makes up more than ninety percent of the universe?"

"Yes," Rhodes said. "Well, dark matter and dark energy."

Maya didn't pursue the dark energy part. "But we know it's there only because of gravity?"

He nodded. "There's just not enough baryonic matter to account for the gravity needed to hold a galaxy together. At least, not given how we currently understand gravity."

She was quiet, thinking.

"I can't believe you're talking about dark matter," Rhodes said. "Keep going, I'm getting turned on."

Maya thought her relationship with Gildas-Joseph would have to be like dark matter and be detectable only by its effects on visible matter. The dark matter of her affair would explain the anomalies in observed galactic rotation—in this case, Maya being pushed closer to Rhodes—but only she would be aware of it. Never Rhodes. Maya was certain of that.

They made love for the last time in Gildas-Joseph's house, on an ugly bare mattress the movers had left behind. The buttons of the mattress poked Maya painfully in the back. Sometimes she thought the whole course of their affair could be charted by the uncomfortable surfaces her back had been pressed against—not that she'd minded.

The mattress was in a back bedroom, and ancient horizontal blinds hung in the windows, crooked and useless. The room was filled with late-afternoon sunshine, and swarming with dust motes. The air was so thick and still and sepia-colored that it reminded Maya of stagnant water.

She could not concentrate enough to come. Gildas-Joseph did, but he didn't tell her a come fact afterward. They dressed slowly. Always before they had hurried into their clothes, laughing, talking, happy in the knowledge that they would see each other within a day or two.

Now Gildas-Joseph tucked in his shirt and said, "I could visit—"

Maya shook her head. "I don't want it to be like that."

"I know." He sighed.

They hugged good-bye in front hall. Hugging seemed peculiar to Maya, not something you did with lovers. With lovers, you kissed and you put your arms around each other, you had sex and you held hands, you spooned and you sat on the other person's lap, and sometimes you scrunched into a bathtub together. But you didn't hug, not precisely. It seemed to be a step that lovers skipped over. Now she understood why. Hugging meant the end.

Maya drove over to Rhodes's parents' house and parked in the driveway. The manic energy that had possessed her for months was suddenly gone. How would she get through this evening? How would she get through all the days that followed?

She stepped out of the car. She could hear voices in the backyard and smell smoke from the barbecue. It had been a cool spring and it seemed too chilly and dark to eat outside but she headed that way.

A tall wooden fence surrounded the backyard and as Maya walked along it toward the gate, she could hear Magellan's voice saying, "Dad, could you, like, actually cook the steaks through this time?"

"They're better rare," Desmond said.

How many years had they been having this conversation? Maya wondered.

"Well, at least don't spoon the blood up from the platter and drink it," Magellan said. "That's so gross."

"It's not blood," Desmond said. "It's meat juice."

"I kind of have to agree with Magellan here," Rhodes's voice said. "Or at least do it inside in the kitchen when you're alone."

"You could get Ebola from doing that," Magellan said.

"Ebola!" Rhodes hooted. "You mean *E. coli*. Sometimes I really think we brought the wrong baby home from the hospital."

"Rhodes, honestly," Hazelene said mildly. "What a thing to say."

Maya came to the end of the fence and was just about to go around the corner of the house into the backyard when her cell phone beeped. She stopped and rooted around in her bag for it. It was a text message from Gildas-Joseph. He had never sent her a text message before. Maya paused and then pressed the button to view it: *Did you know that when someone literally dies of a broken heart, it is called takotsubo cardiomyopathy, because the left ventricle balloons and resembles a tako-tsubo, a Japanese octopus trap?*

A final come fact. Sorrow swept over Maya like a cold north wind. Oh, my love. She closed her eyes and held her cell phone gently to her sternum.

"Maya?"

She opened her eyes. Rhodes was standing in front of her, obviously on his way into the house, probably for more beer.

"What's wrong?" he asked. He gestured to her cell phone. "Did you get bad news?"

"It's just—" Maya's voice failed her and she had to start again. She did not have the presence of mind to lie. "It's just a good-bye message from Gildas-Joseph."

"*Ah, chérie,*" Rhodes said immediately in a Pepé Le Pew voice.

Maya said nothing and Rhodes looked at her. She felt him studying every detail of her expression. He stepped forward and put his arms around her. Maya leaned against his chest. He stroked her hair and he said again, this time in his normal voice, his Rhodes voice, the voice Maya loved best in all the world, "*Ah, chérie.*"

CRANBERRY RELISH

Josie agrees to meet Billy at the coffee shop midway between their houses, about an hour's drive away, and hurries out to the car wearing jeans and a flannel shirt, pausing only long enough for mascara. One year ago, she set off to meet him at the same coffee shop wearing a white blouse, red skirt, black boots, and a tiny lace bra that could barely contain her breasts. One year ago, her hands were so cold that she had trouble grasping the steering wheel. One year ago—you know, Josie's a writer but even she is getting tired of this one-year-ago device. Let's just agree that one year ago, things were different. Then, Josie was going to meet Billy for the first time. She had fallen in love with him online, this stranger who lived two hours away and who she never would have known existed without Facebook. He was in her life only because she "liked" a comment he wrote on someone else's page and he "liked" her "like" and—oh, please, don't get Josie started on the evils of Facebook.

When Josie pushes open the door to the coffee shop and sees Billy sitting in the corner booth, she has the same feeling she has every summer when she sees her nieces and nephews after a yearlong break: shock and fascination and a sort of disbelief. They do exist! And so does Billy.

He is a compact muscular man with very short, prematurely silver hair and startling blue eyes and teeth as white and square as Chiclets. He looks like an actor playing a building contractor, or maybe just the kind of building contractor you would be really happy to have, but he is actually the sales rep for a software company.

He always wears blue or purple dress shirts with white collars (Josie is certain he is aware of what those colors do for his eyes and hair). Today's shirt is cobalt blue, so vivid that it seems to bleed into the air around him. Actually, *all* of Billy seems to bleed into the air around him, as though he is truly larger than life.

Josie has a husband, of course she does. His name is Nathaniel and he's uncommonly tall and broad-shouldered, with a long, handsome, seamed face. A sort of good-looking Herman Munster.

Last night, Nathaniel was standing in the kitchen, reading the mail, when Josie came out of her office and she wrapped her arms around his waist and leaned against him, as though he were a redwood tree. He kissed the top of her head and read to her from the letter in his hand, which was from their son Mickey's school. " '*Your child has been selected as our Student of the Month for demonstrating respect, integrity, dedication, and excellence.*' Do you think we got someone else's letter?"

Josie laughed, and together they checked the name on the envelope and yes, it really and truly was meant for them. They were so lucky—*Josie* was so lucky, and she knew it, too. It was just that she forgot back there for a little while.

· ·

When Billy sees Josie, he says, "You look good." Josie has noticed that men say this to women a lot (though she hardly ever hears a woman say it to a man), and it can mean one of two things. It can mean *You look so good that I'd fuck you right now if I thought you'd let me,* or it can mean, *You look good—well-rested, clear-skinned, like you drink enough water.* If you don't look either sexy *or* healthy, then men say something else, maybe "What do you make of the situation in the Ukraine?" Josie's not too sure because she pretty much always gets the "You look good." She's fortunate like that.

Josie's sons are teenagers now, thirteen and fifteen, and bear no resemblance to the chubby, chuckly babies or the sweet-faced little boys she loved to kiss and cuddle. In fact, they barely resemble humans anymore. They have entered some alarming pupa stage where they grunt at her, and speak in deep voices, and peer out from under their hair like badgers from under a rock. Kit and Mickey (she named them Christopher and Mitchell and now they go by Kit and Mickey—how did *that* happen?) spend all their time over at the neighbor's house or in their rooms with the doors closed, and when Josie enters, they go completely silent while she collects the dirty dishes and delivers clean laundry. What happened to their happy chatter? Josie hopes this phase will end and they will emerge as sociable young men who like to discuss current affairs with her, but she knows in her heart that even when they are, say, twenty and twenty-two, they will only mumble, "Yeah, Ma" in bored voices, waiting for her to leave so their friends can carry cases of beer through the back door.

• •

Josie is not quite sure how to greet Billy, so she ends up shaking his hand like someone from the chamber of commerce, and he looks amused.

She sits down across from him and he watches as she takes off her jacket and flips her hair back over shoulders. She had forgotten that—how he watches everything she does, like she is the most fascinating person in the world. She has a moment of longing: it was a wonderful feeling.

The waitress comes and Josie orders a cup of coffee and then she and Billy lean slightly forward, exactly like two people who don't want to be overheard.

"So what's up?" she asks.

Billy rolls his shoulders and runs his hand over the top of his head. She knows what he's going to say even before he says it. "I've met someone."

Josie's next-door neighbor is a woman named Maricella, which is so close to *varicella* that Josie started thinking of her as Chicken Pox and now she can't stop. Chicken Pox and her husband have four sons, all of them teenagers, and their house doesn't just have nods to the teenage lifestyle, like Josie's does, with the extra fridge in the garage and the super-strength laundry detergent—their house has made big, structural, central concessions to the teenage lifestyle, like a hot tub and a pool table and a sound system and a game room. It is without a doubt Kit and Mickey's favorite place to be, and every other boy in the neighborhood's favorite place, too. Josie doesn't know how Chicken Pox survives over there, but she's grateful to her, and so is everyone else. Josie has noticed that people are always giving Chicken Pox gifts—houseplants and baked goods and bottles of wine—the way that they might pay monthly dues at a community center, or perhaps make small offerings to some minor goddess.

Chicken Pox herself is not very goddess-like. She is a small woman with oversize glasses and limp wavy brown hair. She is the most literal person Josie has ever met and when Josie says something like, "The supermarket was a little slice of hell this morning," Chicken Pox looks profoundly puzzled but Josie supposes that that's what happens to you after a lifetime of making sandwiches.

When Billy says he's met someone, there's a very slight dropping sensation in Josie's rib cage, like the clunk inside a freezer when the icemaker releases another cube. But it's almost imperceptible. You would have to be standing with your ear pressed right up against her chest to hear it. She's certain it doesn't show on her face.

"Her name is Paisley," Billy says. "And she's lovely. Paisley is lovely." He seems to like her saying her name, which is remarkable because if Josie had a lover named Paisley, she would never ever say her name out loud, not even if Paisley were about to step in front of a truck.

"How did you meet?" Josie asks.

Billy sighs. "We haven't actually *met,*" he says. "I got to know her on Twitter."

Twitter, yes. Josie and Billy met on Facebook but Paisley and Billy met on Twitter because times are changing, and if you don't believe that, you haven't noticed how many people eat kale now.

. .

What did Josie think when she saw Billy for the very first time? That's hard to say. She might not have even actually *seen* him because her own anxiety was like a strong wind in her face, making her eyes water, and the world was a glittering blur.

She only remembers sitting down across from him in this very same coffee shop, and how he held her icy hands with his warm dry ones and said, "What are you so nervous about?"

And Josie had whispered, "Because we're doing this all backwards," meaning, of course, that their minds had fallen in love before their bodies did and what if their bodies got all stubborn and wouldn't fall in line?

"Tell me about Paisley," Josie says to Billy.

Are there words dearer to the heart of someone infatuated? No. Billy beams. "She's married, naturally," he says, as though that should be obvious, which Josie supposes it should be. "And she's thirty-five and she's a math teacher and she has long dark hair and big brown eyes."

"How can you be sure she is who she says she is?" Josie asks. "What if she's really a man or a high school student or a serial killer?"

"You weren't," Billy says.

"No," Josie agrees. "I wasn't."

She is beginning to relax. She still knows how to talk to him.

"Besides, I've seen her on Skype," he says.

Ah, well, *Skype*. He doesn't have to say anything more. She knows without asking that Billy and Paisley aren't on Skype discussing books and movies. She knows exactly what they're on there talking about. Exactly.

Josie and Billy had never had Skype sex but that was only because Josie preferred phone sex and cybersex. Josie is a writer; Josie likes language. Cybersex was kind of *like* writing, actually— spinning a fantasy that touched somebody else, using nothing but your brain and the same words available to everyone. Only, unlike with writing, afterward your eye sockets didn't feel hot and scratchy, and your head didn't ache, and you didn't worry that you'd never had an original thought or that your characters were boring, and you didn't wonder if you were an untalented hack and wish you'd gone to dental school after all. The worst that would happen with cybersex is that you came so hard you slipped into a vegetable type of mental state and backed over Chicken Pox's mailbox when you drove off to collect the boys from school but even that wasn't so bad.

"Paisley and I are supposed to meet next weekend," Billy says, "but I'm not sure I'll go through with it."

Now here's something Josie knows the answer to, although he hasn't asked a question: of course he'll go through with it, of course he will meet her. Once you decide to do it, to make that leap from virtual to physical, nothing can hold you back, no matter how much you might debate it or rethink it or tell yourself you won't go. Josie should know. It's as inevitable as—as—as the white breath of the buffalo in the wintertime, or some other Native American proverb, if they have them about Internet dating.

· ·

Once, late at night, when Josie and Billy were chatting on Face-book, Josie had typed *What will happen when we meet, do you think?* Not because she had the slightest question about what would happen, but because she wanted to hear him say it.

I will make love to you, Billy typed back, *and as soon as I'm able, we'll do it again.*

That was very sexy to Josie, that being able bit. Because it implied a period of wanting to and *not* being able, which was to Josie the essence of their whole relationship: wanting to and not being able.

"Did you tell Paisley about me?" Josie asks.

"Oh, no," Billy says, looking shocked. "No, no, no."

Has Josie mentioned that dishonesty is one of Billy's worst qualities? Not to mention being bad at it?

Of course he told Paisley. After all, he told Josie about the lover before her: a redheaded woman he'd gone to high school with named Lisa who worked as a paralegal in Boston. The only other things Josie knew about her was that they used to meet while Lisa's husband thought Lisa was at handbell choir practice and that Lisa broke off their affair.

Josie would like to believe that Billy told Paisley that he had been involved with an incredibly poised woman who wrote haunting short stories and had sexy shadows at the corners of her mouth when she smiled. She would like to believe that, but she doesn't. Probably he said she gave good blow jobs and bad hand jobs and left it at that.

. .

Do you know how many women there are in Boston named Lisa who work as paralegals and have red hair and potentially went to Billy's high school? Neither does Josie, but it's a really high number. And Josie found her! Josie found Billy's Lisa using Google and Facebook and with a level of resourcefulness MacGyver could only have dreamed of. When she found Lisa—she knew for certain it was the right Lisa because she belonged to a Facebook handbell group called the Embellishments—Josie could only stare at the computer screen, at this woman with auburn hair tucked demurely behind her ears and a formal expression. This woman who had been Billy's lover, who had given up what Josie desired more than anything in the world. Josie had felt light-headed and shaky, the room seemed to shimmer, and it felt like her heart was trying to climb up her throat with thick webbed feet.

It would be easy to search for Paisley, given the uniqueness (and unfortunateness) of her name and the fact that she must follow Billy on Twitter. But Josie doesn't have to find her—she already knows Paisley as well as she knows herself.

Josie's not an idiot, though it's hard to believe that sometimes. She questions it now, but she questioned it then, too: Was it really possible to fall in love with someone who was only the equivalent of strokes on a keyboard? Well, of course it was. Didn't Josie love Stephen King? William Shakespeare? Dr. Seuss? Not to mention Rhett Butler, who didn't even have the advantage of the strokes on a keyboard.

Online at least, Billy made her laugh, and feel good about

herself, and examine her own life more closely, and he helped her tolerate disappointments and rejection letters, and he celebrated her achievements, and even her children's achievements, and the idea of him touching another woman made Josie's pupils dilate and her fingers clench, and wasn't that love? Wasn't it?

Whenever Josie spent time over at Chicken Pox's house, and then came home and saw Nathaniel, she drank in the sight of him with a deep satisfaction and relief—someone smart who got her jokes! Actually, she used to feel the same way when she saw Nathaniel after being with Billy.

But for someone so intelligent, Nathaniel seems to have a strange tolerance—even liking—for Chicken Pox. He once actually suggested that they have Chicken Pox and her husband over for dinner, a prospect Josie regarded with only marginally more enthusiasm than the collapse of industrial society. How could Nathaniel have wanted that? How could he be married to Josie and have wanted that?

"What really worries me is Kimberly finding out," Billy says.

Josie wraps her hands around her coffee mug. "Well, she's bound to, sooner or later." This is something she believes, although it didn't happen to her. But there's a limit on how much late-night computer activity you can pass off as online Christmas shopping or NFL picks. People catch on.

"Yikes," says Billy, looking startled, and Josie can tell that he hasn't considered Kimberly finding out a real possibility, but more of a theoretical one, the way Peter Higgs must have thought about that elementary particle for all those years.

Kimberly is Billy's wife, obviously. Josie once knew a whole roster of facts about her but all she really remembers now is her exercise schedule, which she knew only slightly less well than she knew her own children's birthdays: Body Pump on Mondays at five; Zumba on Tuesdays at five-thirty; Spinning on Wednesdays and Thursdays at six; Strong, Stretched, and Balanced on Fridays at four-thirty; and a lovely long two-hour yoga session on Saturday mornings. Solid blocks of time when Josie and Billy could have phone sex. Josie hopes now that at least the poor woman *liked* to exercise. At least maybe, in a way, they were all happy there for a little while.

Somewhere between Josie's second and third cup of coffee, Billy leans across the table and takes her hand. What's surprising—shocking, really—about this is that right at that moment Josie is wondering what to make for supper. For months and months Josie thought about Billy when she should have been wondering what to make for supper—or what to say at Kit's parent-teacher conference or where Mickey's lunch card was or if she left the oven on—and now here she is *with* Billy, and all she can think about is whether she used the last of the onions the night before. (She's pretty sure she did.) It's the kind of reversal Josie would struggle with in fiction, but look at her right now in real life, doing it perfectly.

Here are the things Josie knows about Paisley. She knows that the day Paisley is supposed to meet Billy is imprinted in Paisley's mind in glowing letters, and if Paisley sees that same date on something, like a milk carton or a PTA letter, she feels a jolt of connection. She knows that Paisley is planning for every con-tingency, like a member of the White House press office: what will happen if her car breaks down, or her children get sick, or her mother-in-law dies, or she gets her period. And Paisley is planning outfits, too, or more likely buying new ones, which is always a mistake—you never look good in brand-new clothes; they give off an anxious vibe all by themselves—but one Josie couldn't stop herself from making either. Josie knows that no matter what Paisley weighs, she's currently dieting, and she knows that at a certain point she will stop dieting either because she's too hungry to keep it up or so she won't look drawn, but she'll probably keep exercising until the very last minute. And on the day itself, she'll obsess over her handbag and earrings and nail polish and lipstick color and all those little things instead of concentrating on her basic sexiness, which is all men have ever cared about or ever will.

In the days before she met Billy for the first time, Josie was so happy that she agreed to help Chicken Pox with the Friends of the Library Used Book Sale and spent an entire afternoon stack-ing and sorting the kinds of awful books that Josie hadn't known still existed: obscure, cheap paperbacks with yellow-edged pages and print as tiny as flea dirt.

Toward the end of the afternoon, some woman called Chicken Pox's cell phone to say she couldn't work the morning shift of the book sale and then Chicken Pox called about eight different people and rejiggered the whole schedule and finally got someone to cover that shift if someone *else* picked up that woman's kid from karate practice.

And Josie, who felt during those months that she was living

the most exciting life imaginable, said to Chicken Pox, "I think it's kind of amazing how much of our lives are spent having conversations about drop-off and pickup and traffic circles and phone plans and, I don't know, the difficulty of finding a really good electrician and the best recipe for cranberry relish."

"Cranberry relish?" Chicken Pox said, perplexed. "Do you put cloves in that?"

Before they met, Billy used to say to Josie, "Imagine us having sex. Think how *good* it would feel." Josie liked the simplicity of that. They would have sex; it would feel good. He made it sound healthy and wholesome and sensible, like a camping trip or maybe oatmeal cookies.

But in reality the sex had been awkward. Maybe because of all that phone sex, they weren't prepared for the actual nitty-gritty of it: Josie's high-heeled boots had made her an inch taller than Billy, his feet had tangled in his jeans when he took them off, she had banged her elbow on the headboard. Billy had thrust into her forever—his back growing wet and slippery under Josie's hands—until finally he came with a deep sigh, like someone setting down a heavy box. Josie had never heard a man sigh during sex before and she realized abruptly that she had just fucked a stranger. It made her want to cry. Really, it was nothing like oatmeal cookies at all.

Billy is still holding her hand. Josie has long skinny fingers and he strokes them gently, pulling on each one. Despite the bad sex, Josie had always liked that about him—the way he paid attention to every part of her body, not just the usual ones.

"Sweet Josie," Billy says. This is something he used to write when they chatted on Facebook, and it used to seem so expressive to Josie, like the literary equivalent of a moan. It was almost unbearably heady to know that she had stirred a man to moan on the Internet.

The only thing worse than the first time they had sex was the second time they had sex. Of course they had sex a second time (and a third and a fourth)—what else were they going to do with all that emotion, all that passion that swirled around them like the vapor from an open refrigerator? But by the second time, Josie knew it was over. She knew they wouldn't see each other for long, and she also knew that she couldn't go back to being who she was before she met Billy. She was no longer the happy, lucky woman who had juggled husband and lover for so many months. She was just a boring fool who'd had sex with a man who sometimes wrote *defiantly* when he meant *definitely*. By the time Josie sat on the edge of the bed afterward and began pulling on her clothes, she was already trying to figure out how to be a third person, some other person who'd left all this behind.

In the days right after Josie and Billy had sex for the fourth and last time, Chicken Pox called to tell her that Diet Coke was on sale at the supermarket, two packs for ten dollars, and this put Josie in such a black mood that she *lied* and told Chicken Pox that she got a better deal at the supermarket way outside of town and Chicken Pox said, "Oh, my God! The twelve-packs or the twenty-four-packs?" and Josie said the twenty-four-packs, and

Chicken Pox made a distressed sound and said, "How much did you pay?" and Josie told her three dollars per pack, and Chicken Pox said in a sad voice, "But you probably didn't save all that much, when you figure in the price of gas driving there," and Josie hung up because she was about to say that she had had a fifty-percent-off coupon for gas, which is, like, impossible, as far as Josie knows, and of course none of this was Chicken Pox's fault anyway.

"You know something strange?" Josie says. She has fallen back into the habit of drawing out every exchange, the way they used to do on Facebook. Back when they prolonged every discussion to extract the most possible pleasure from it: *You know what? . . . You'll think I'm crazy. . . . I'm in love with you. . . . I really am.*

"What?" Billy asks.

"I'm happy for you, about Paisley," Josie says. And it's true. Or at least it's more true than it's not true.

It takes a second, but Billy lets go of her hand and takes a sip of his coffee, although it must be cold now.

"I'll let you know what happens," he says finally.

Maybe he means it spitefully, as a little payback, but Josie doesn't think so. He probably just will honestly want to tell her. She'll know how it goes for Billy and Paisley whether she wants to or not, and right now she's not sure she cares so much about the ending, like those unfinished novels Josie wrote before she decided she was a short-story writer and gave up on all that.

· ·

On the drive home, Josie thinks that if she sees Billy dispassion-ately now, it means that she once saw him passionately, and Josie has never heard that phrase before. But it's true. She used to see Billy through passionate lenses—sort of a combination of rose-colored glasses and beer goggles. He was so desirable to Josie that she believed everyone he met must be instantly drawn to him. She used to be so envious of the people he came into casual contact with—the neighbor he went running with, the mother who drove in the same carpool, the woman at work who han-dled accounts, the lucky girl who served his coffee. All those people who saw him every day and experienced the magic of his presence.

But today she saw only a moderately handsome man, one who talks a lot and watches her face to see if anything he says is hitting the mark. She sees him so clearly now that she could go home and write a story about him.

When Josie pulls into her driveway, Chicken Pox is standing there in front of her, like one of those cardboard cutouts of pedestrians who pop up on driving courses. Josie is very tempted to run Chicken Pox over and see if she springs back up, but she's standing too close to the garage.

Josie gets out of her car and Chicken Pox tells her that her minivan was broken into last night and the thieves took all her parking change and her mixed CDs and a carton of homemade canned goods Chicken Pox was planning to take to the church bring-and-buy sale.

"That's terrible," Josie says, but she wonders if this means that somewhere a man in a ski mask is eating watermelon pickles and listening to Meat Loaf's "Not a Dry Eye in the House." She hopes so.

Nathaniel's car pulls up behind Josie's and he and the boys arrive just in time for Chicken Pox to tell them that she has already alerted the police and the neighborhood watch but that they should be sure to lock their cars.

"Why don't you come in and have a glass of wine?" Nathaniel asks.

"Well, okay," Chicken Pox says, "but I can't stay long because I'm making sloppy joes for supper."

Josie feels a little pang of envy—Chicken Pox makes *wonderful* sloppy joes.

They go inside and it's all business as usual with Nathaniel pouring drinks and Josie rummaging for supper ingredients and Kit and Mickey kicking off their shoes and picking grapes out of the fruit bowl. The only difference is that Chicken Pox is sitting at their kitchen table drinking red wine.

Josie turns on the oven and takes some pork chops out of the freezer and then she sits at the table, too. Chicken Pox sees the Student of the Month letter stuck on the refrigerator and gives them the lowdown on the principal of Mickey's school, or what would be the lowdown if it contained anything gossipy or scandalous or even mildly interesting. And then Chicken Pox says that she and her husband and all four of her sons are going to volunteer at a soup kitchen this weekend and she was wondering if Kit and Mickey would like to come along.

"No way," Kit says through a mouthful of grapes. Josie loves him; oh, she loves him.

But Mickey says, "Will we be done in time to watch *Family Guy*?"

"I'm sure we will," Chicken Pox says.

"I'd like to join you," Nathaniel says.

Goodness. Are those sloppy joes over there making themselves?

But Josie doesn't say that. She just refills Chicken Pox's glass while Chicken Pox and Nathaniel have a long complicated logistical discussion about whose car to take.

Josie thinks that the problem with being a writer is that you miss a lot of your life wondering if the things that happen to you are good enough to use in a story, and most of the time they're not and you have to make shit up anyway.

So Josie tries not to go somewhere else in her head. She stays right here. She stays right here in the conversation like someone standing on a rock in the middle of rising creek, because conversations like these are the only kind she has now.

THOUGHTS OF A BRIDESMAID

At the Airport

Haley must have come straight from the hospital. She's wearing scrubs. To top it off, she shrieks, "There you are!" as soon as she sees me, like she's been called to the airport to give me a life-saving shot of adrenaline.

We hug in front of the baggage claim. Her shoulders are so thin it feels like I could break them with my hands. "Oh, Fern," she says.

She insists on hauling my suitcase off the conveyor belt even though it's very heavy and she practically cripples the man next to her by hitting him in the legs with it.

In the car, she tells me about an obscene phone call she got last week. She doesn't ask me how school is and I don't ask her how work is. That's the way we are.

At the Hairdresser's

This is a dry run. Haley is big on dry runs. She used to pack up her car with empty boxes and suitcases about a week before she actually moved out of the dorm just to make sure everything would fit. I'm surprised she's not having a rehearsal rehearsal.

The guy does Haley's hair in about two seconds. He just whips it up on top of her head and it looks terrific, the right number of wisps falling around her face.

Then he tries to do mine and keeps sighing. Haley sits in the other chair, making suggestions.

Finally the guy says, "Look, I just can't get it to do that. Her bangs grow *up*."

"Up?" Haley says.

"It's like she was conceived in a gravity booth or something," the guy tells her, winking.

Haley smiles. The guy smiles. If his hands weren't stuck in my hair, I would probably get up and excuse myself.

This happens all the time. Haley and I used to study together in the science library and men would ask her out and foreign students would ask me how to use the card catalog.

On Meeting Haley's Fiancé

Pear Man. That's what he's shaped like, a giant pear. He's wearing white sweats that hug his hips. If only they were a nice golden color, the image would be complete.

"Hi, Fern," he says.

"Hi," I say.

That is basically all we have to say to each other. Pear Man checks his watch and says he has to get back to the bank. This is his lunch hour and he used it to go jogging, he explains to me.

"Oh," I say.

Haley looks amused.

On Meeting Haley's Lover

"This is Tony," says Haley, which is funny because that's exactly what she said when she introduced me to Pear Man, whose name is also Tony. I could call them Tony One and Tony Two if I hadn't already named Pear Man. I guess I can still call this one Tony Two.

"Nice to meet you," Tony Two's head says. That's all I can see of him; he's standing in the bushes outside the family room window. At first I thought he was the gardener, but it turns out that he and Haley meet this way. He just runs up and looks in the window and if she's there waiting for him, they open the window and agree to meet somewhere.

This other friend of mine, Evelyn, is having an affair with a married man. Evelyn and this man call each other at pay phones at predetermined times and when they do get together, they drive around for two hours and switch cars three times. Haley would never waste her time like that.

Tony Two is tall and slender, with a big nose that is somehow attractive. He's a paramedic. He met Haley giving blood. "I'll see you later," Haley says to him. She leans down and kisses his forehead.

On the Maid of Honor

Haley asked me first, but I told her that I would only take enough time off school to be in the wedding and I wouldn't be able to throw showers or anything, so she chose her sister, Anna.

Anna has Haley's eyes, but not quite, and bad skin. I know she must think of herself as the brainy one. I think of myself this way, so of course we are rivals.

In the Dressing Room

Probably there are lots of black bridesmaid's dresses and lots of backless bridesmaid's dresses, but I don't think there are an awful lot of backless black bridesmaid's dresses.

I look at myself in the mirror. I look like an unsuccessful prostitute. Haley throws open the door of the dressing room. She is wearing a bra and the hoops of her wedding dress.

"Oh, my God!" she yells. "You look terrific!"

The other people in the shop look over at us. There's a man here and he looks at Haley with interest. I yank her inside the dressing room, which isn't easy considering the size of her hoops, and shut the door.

Haley pokes my chest. "I don't think we even need to alter it." I read once that brides ask their homeliest friends to be bridesmaids so that they look better by comparison.

Now Haley's mother pulls the door open. I'm glad Haley's the one wearing only a bra.

"Oh, girls." Haley's mother sighs in the doorway. "Black. I still can't get over it."

"I should wear black," Haley says, putting her arms around my waist and leaning against me. The hoops rustle and the material of the black dress makes a crushing noise. "I shouldn't even pretend to be pure."

In Haley's Bathroom

Haley's bathroom is pink, with pink tiles and pink towels and rugs and toothbrushes and cups and even one of those pink shaggy covers on the toilet. It is also the only room with a lock on the door. "So," says Haley. "What do you say?"

She is leaning against the sink, wearing her bathrobe. Tony Two is sitting on the pink rug, fingering the hem of her robe. He climbed up on the porch roof and came in Haley's bathroom window. I am sitting on the edge of the bathtub, the track of the pink-tinted glass door biting into my legs.

"Sure," I say.

Haley grins at me. So does Tony Two. It is like the moment in movies when people should kiss, but confusing. Should Haley kiss me because I've agreed to pretend Tony Two is my boyfriend? Should Haley kiss Tony Two because now he can be at her wedding? Should I kiss Tony Two for practice?

My Theory on Why Haley Is Marrying Pear Man

Basically, Pear Man's appeal is that he looks like an Easter Island statue. Haley's just perpetuating her nursing image. People will admire her for marrying this homely person and assume he has a heart of gold and that Haley's nurturing brought out his true nature or something.

The problem here is that Pear Man's true nature is just about what it appears to be. My God, the man is a repossession officer. Besides, only Miss Kitty on *Gunsmoke* truly has a heart of gold.

My Theory on Why Haley Keeps Tony Two

Actually, it could be for a lot of reasons, like this friend of my mother's who had an affair with a man who went to museums with her because her husband would never go to museums with her. It could be something like that.

But more likely, she just likes the idea of Pear Man finding out.

On Days Haley Spent in Bed

The first kind were days when she didn't have classes or just didn't feel like going and she would lie in bed and call my name until I woke up and went staggering into her room.

"I'm not getting up today," she would say, patting the bed. "Come here, let's order something."

We would order pizza or Chinese food and Haley wouldn't even get out of bed when the delivery boys came to the door. She just shouted, "Come in!" as loud as she could and then she paid them right there in her bedroom, flirting with them, the whites of her eyes as bright as her Snoopy T-shirt.

The other kind of days she spent in bed, she was too depressed to call me and she wouldn't always speak to me. Sometimes, I sat on the edge of the bed and brushed her hair. Other times, I sat in the chair in the corner of her room, not daring to leave her alone, looking at how thin her neck was as she lay facing the wall.

In Haley's Dead Brother's Room

Haley's mother would like people to think that his room is exactly as he left it. His high school track trophies are on the dresser and his college pennant is on the wall. His yearbook is even open on his desk, like at a tourist attraction, Monticello or Laura Ingalls's log cabin, where the desk always has an unfinished letter angled so the visitors can read it.

Haley told me once that this is a joke. Her brother had dropped out of college two years before he died and worked at an automotive parts store. "He didn't even have a college yearbook," she told me. "My mother sent away for that."

Sleeping here is odd, but it's not what you might think. This is, after all, the room nearest Haley's; this is where she wants me. In a way, I feel very loved.

On the Night Before the Night Before the Wedding

I wake up and Haley is in my bed, tucked against my body like spoons in a stack.

"What are you doing here?" I whisper.

Haley sighs. "Do that thing with my hair," she says, keeping her back to me.

I untangle my hand from the sheets and stroke her hair away from her face. The ends of her hair brush my arms.

"That feels good," she says after a minute. Her voice is slow. I am putting her to sleep. "I miss this."

On Why Pear Man Hates Me

I have absolutely no idea.

Actually, that's not true, although I would like to think it were, so I could act baffled and wounded. He hates me because once when Haley was visiting me, he tried to call her every hour on the hour for sixteen straight hours and sixteen times I told him she was in the shower. I don't even remember now who she was with.

On Why I Hate Pear Man

I hate him because he doesn't get my jokes.

Yesterday, he stopped by again after jogging. He must be trying to get in shape before the wedding. He was wearing green sweatpants this time and the kind of headphones that have antennae sticking up from them. He looked like an air traffic controller. "Have you been landing planes?" I said to him, and he said, "What?"

That kind of joke doesn't hold up well if you have to explain it and so you can see why I don't feel guilty about him.

With Haley's Mother Making a Salad

If you're not thin when you come to Haley's house, you are when you leave. Once when I was here, they served tomatoes for lunch. So I'm helping to make the salad and every once in a while, I eat a handful of bacon bits.

"I hope you and Haley can go to Daytona Beach again during your spring break," Haley's mother says to me. "She had so much fun."

I nod. I continue cutting cheddar cheese into tiny cubes. I eat one of the cubes. "That would be great," I say.

I have never been to Daytona Beach.

Things Haley Taught Me

Vitamin C won't prevent you from catching a cold, but it will help you get rid of one faster.

Wet your hands when you pull on panty hose and you're less likely to snag them.

Men have a harder time unfastening bras that hook in the front.

In the Backyard

Haley, Anna, and I are on lawn chairs, trying to get tan for tomorrow. Anna is reading a book. I don't ask her what she is reading because I know it will turn out to be by Voltaire or somebody.

Haley is telling me about one of her patients at the hospital. "He told me that he divides women into four groups, and I'm in the pony group."

"The pony group?"

"Yes, well, apparently all the groups are kinds of horses," Haley says. "I guess I should take it as a compliment that I'm not a brood mare or something."

When we were roommates, Haley made me go to anatomy lab with her on visitor's day.

"Isn't this interesting?" she kept saying, showing me the body of a burn victim they called Aunt Jemima.

"Yes," I said, holding my coat over my nose and mouth to combat the smell of formaldehyde.

Haley snapped on a pair of surgical gloves and groped around in one of the sliced-open legs. "I want to show you this muscle," she said. "It looks just like a ribbon."

In Haley's Bathroom Again

Haley got a sunburn and now she's taking a long cool bath, hoping it will fade. I am sitting on the toilet, keeping her company and painting my toenails.

The bad thing about painting your toenails is that unless you're organized, you never get around to removing the nail polish and it takes about six months to chip off. Still, I paint my big toenail with red polish as I say to Haley, "Who did you go to Daytona Beach with?" Haley gathers her hair up on top of her head, where it shines like a garbage bag. She wrings the water out of it and looks at me. She doesn't ask how I know. She says, "Someone from work."

I say, "Oh."

Then I say, "You know, you don't have to—"

"Look, don't you start," Haley says, stretching and letting her hair fall back into the water. "Not you."

On the Present Haley Gives Me

"You always seemed so taken with it," Haley says. "If you mind having something secondhand, I can get you something else."

"No," I say. "I mean, no, this is fine."

Haley had always claimed that the ring was just a piece of jewelry like any other, that it had no special significance. It's a large clear sapphire with two tiny diamonds on either side of it and a boy gave it to Haley once as a promise ring. Although she no longer even kept in touch with this boy by the time she was my roommate, Haley still wore the ring.

Two different boys have given me rings. I tossed the first down our kitchen sink in a fit of anger and dramatically flipped the switch to the disposal. Our disposal never worked quite right after that and my father spent a lot of hours working on it, saying, "I wish I knew what got stuck down here. Did someone drop a spoon?" The second ring I wrapped in blue tissue paper and tucked away in a small wooden box that also contains one of my baby teeth. It seems to me that either of these is better than just wearing the thing around. If I had been given a promise ring from a boy who broke up with me, I would have mailed the ring back to him jammed on a severed chicken's foot.

"Thank you," I say to Haley, hugging her. I slip the ring on my finger, where it twinkles dully, heavy as an heirloom.

My Revised Theory on Why Haley Keeps Tony Two

Now that Haley also has this person from work that she went to Daytona Beach with, she can worry about being caught by her fiancé *and* her lover.

While Getting Ready for the Rehearsal Dinner

"Now I know why I never did this before," Haley says, sweeping my face with her makeup brushes.

"Why?"

"Because it is absolutely disgusting the way your eyes are twitching."

"I can't help it," I say. "I have very sensitive eyes."

"Oh, my God," Haley says, stepping back. "I knew if I put eyeliner on you, you'd be prettier than me."

I look in the mirror. There is not enough eyeliner in the world to make me prettier than Haley. I don't think there are even operations that could do that. Still, I wonder why she didn't tell me sooner.

On How Haley's Brother Died

It was a freak accident. He was skiing and hit a tree, but that's not what killed him. He was knocked out and suffocated underneath the snow.

What's even more awful is that his girlfriend practically had a breakdown last year. Now once a month, she and Haley meet for lunch and talk about Haley's brother.

"Isn't that depressing?" I ask Haley.

"Oh, not really," she says. "It's just something I can do for her."

At the Rehearsal Dinner

I am supposed to sit next to Haley, but Pear Man changes places with her so we can sit boy-girl, boy-girl. He actually says that. If he and Haley have children, they will hate him.

Haley switches places with him during dessert.

"Do you remember," I say, scraping at the bottom of my mousse dish, "how you used to want to live in London for a year?"

Haley hands me the rest of her mousse.

"I still do," she says. "You can live in my kitchen and sell Avon or something."

"What about Tony?" I say.

"Part One or Part Two?" Haley asks. That's how much alike we think.

After the Rehearsal Dinner

Someday, Haley's father will probably shoot Tony Two, thinking he's a prowler. Haley is talking to him in a low voice through the family room window.

"Fern, come here," she whispers. She hands me her shoes and her earrings and slings her legs over the windowsill. She is still wearing the dress from the rehearsal.

Tony Two grasps Haley's waist as she slides out. "See you later, Fern." He winks. I imagine them twenty years from now, Haley married to Pear Man, Tony Two backing his ambulance up to their family room window every couple of days.

"I'll be back in an hour," Haley says.

I feel like I should hand her a sack lunch. Instead, I shut the window behind her.

On the Night Before the Wedding

I hold Haley's head above the toilet while she throws up for the hundredth time. About an hour ago, I braided her hair to keep it out of the way.

Her forehead sags against my hands.

"Haley?" I whisper. I pull her back and prop her up against the tub. She cries when she's not throwing up and her eyes are swollen to the size of golf balls.

I pull her up and put her to bed.

I sit on the edge of the bed, pressing washcloths soaked in ice water to her eyes so they will not be swollen tomorrow. This is another thing Haley taught me to do.

After half an hour, I bite one of my fingertips and can't feel it, but Haley's skin is still so hot it seems to glow in the dark.

On the Morning of the Wedding

I wake up with a dent in my palm from the sapphire, which had slipped around on my finger.

I am wearing a ring bought by a man I've never met, I'm lying in a dead boy's bed, and my best friend is about to marry a man she doesn't even like. If I concentrate hard enough, these things will snap into a logical pattern.

I go into Haley's room and pause in the doorway. She is twined in her pink sheets. Her face is not puffy, her shoulder is a dark golden brown, her hair shines like fingernail polish. I will never know someone this beautiful again.

On the Way to the Church

Haley and I drive to the church together in her little white Camaro, an early wedding present from Pear Man.

She knew from the beginning what kind of wedding dress she wanted, there was never any agonizing over eggshell satin or ivory lace. She chose yards and yards of billowing white silk and one of those huge headdresses that normally I think are ugly. On Haley, though, it will be gorgeous, and someday I will probably try to imitate it at my own wedding with disastrous results.

I sit in the passenger seat with the atrocious headpiece in my lap, looking at Haley as she drives. She sits on the edge of her seat, chewing her lower lip. To people who glance into the car, she must look like a nervous wreck, but actually, she's always like this at the wheel. She didn't learn to drive until she was twenty. "What are you going to do about Tony Two after you're married?" I ask suddenly.

Haley stops at a red light and examines her lipstick in the rearview mirror. "What do you mean?" she says, a tiny frown between her eyes.

In the Corridor

Tony Two seems to think everyone will believe we are boyfriend and girlfriend if he keeps his hand glued to my back. His fingers slip under the edge of the backless dress. I can't tell whether this is intentional or not, but I keep my arms pressed tightly against my sides.

The Wedding Woman claps her hands at Tony Two and tells him to go sit down. She's this woman who works for the church and supervises us. When it's time for us to walk down the aisle, she'll stand in the doorway and give us each little pats on the back, like starting horses out of a gate.

"Now, girls," she says, after Tony Two leaves. "I've been in more than two hundred weddings. There's nothing to it."

I roll my eyes at Haley and whisper, "She acts like a Veteran of Foreign Wars or something."

Haley laughs. She slips her arms around my neck and I automatically grasp her waist, the folds of her white silk and my black dress pleating together. We sway together for a moment. How many times, at how many parties, did I support Haley like this, while she was drunk and weak with laughter? Parties where I stayed by her for hours, tired and miserable after the effects of the beer wore off. Parties where I stood with my feet aching while Haley flirted and danced and finally left with someone. How could I have forgotten that? Haley always leaves with someone else.

The Wedding Woman frowns and claps her hands. In a minute, she will separate us and send me down the aisle. Right now, that's what I want, for my part to be over, for this wedding to be over, so I can go home.

I lean forward. Haley's head is thrown back, her neck straining under the weight of her hair and veil. Her back arches against my hands and I can feel the knobs of her spine. It must look as though I am about to kiss her in the fashion of silent-film stars, the woman swooning back in passion.

"Hey." I put my mouth next to where her ear must be under the veil. "I have to go."

THE RHETT BUTLERS

You always think of him as Mr. Eagleton, even after you start sleeping with him. You always call him that, too.

You are so naïve, even for a teenager. You actually believe that story about a kid dying from eating Pop Rocks and soda together—you not only believe it, you believe it happened in your town—and that's such an old, old story. But then, so is yours and Mr. Eagleton's.

He is forty, and blandly handsome in the way of homicide detectives, or 1920s bankers. You are almost seventeen. It starts with a kiss by the world map in the back of the classroom after everyone else has gone for the day. You had known this kiss was coming, had encouraged it in all sorts of ways, but still it surprises you.

It surprises you even more the next morning when your best friend from next door, Marcy Hutchins, calls and says, "Mr. Eagleton keeps riding his motorcycle around the court and looking at your house."

You peer out the window, still with the phone to your ear, and sure enough, a motorcycle slowly cruises by, and the helmeted driver turns his head in your direction.

"You should probably do something," Marcy says. "My dad

says he's going to go out and tell him to stop disturbing the peace."

"Okay," you say.

"Also, he's wearing weird jeans," Marcy says, and hangs up.

You tell your parents you're going to the library and hurry outside. You cut through the backyard and intercept Mr. Eagleton as he roars around the block. You climb on the back of his motorcycle and ride away. Probably your parents would be more upset about the fact that you're not wearing a helmet than the fact that you're going off with the history teacher, but only just.

You've always liked school but now you *really* like school, because in addition to the thrill of getting good grades, there's the thrill of seeing Mr. Eagleton. It's like the two interesting parts of your life have combined and now your whole life is interesting, although there's still homework and dinner with your parents and raking leaves and stuff. But school is so *satisfying* now. In class, when Mr. Eagleton makes everyone laugh, you get to sit there, knowing they all love him and he loves only you.

Sometimes you pass each other in the halls and he'll stop talking to whoever he's talking to and say, "Hey, catch me later, I want to talk to you about a project," and you can't believe that nobody realizes you and he only have eyes for each other.

Your friends, the other teachers, the school itself, are all a colorful blur, a soft rich background for the movie that's your life now.

The very next week Mr. Eagleton wants to go to a hotel with you. He is tired of making out in your car and you can't go to his house because it's right across from the school and he has nosy neighbors. But you can't go to the Comfort Inn because Marcy's older brother is the manager and you can't go to the Holiday Inn because sometimes other teachers go there for the lunch buffet. So Mr. Eagleton says he will take you to a motel called the Starlite just outside of town.

"What kind of motel is that?" you ask meekly.

"One with a stained mattress and a naked lightbulb," Mr. Eagleton says. He means to be ironic but the irony is that it's a pretty accurate description.

You know that in the motel room, you and Mr. Eagleton will take off all your clothes and get in bed. You imagine it will lead to something you think of as *naked kissing*. Which it does, but the naked kissing lasts for about five minutes and then becomes sex.

All your life, men will snort with laughter when you tell them about this naked kissing business—about the fact that you actually thought that—but it's true.

The day after you have sex the first time, you wake up with an awful stomachache. It keeps getting worse, and eventually you leave school and have Marcy take you to the doctor, because what else are you going to do—go to the ER holding hands with Mr. Eagleton? Besides, he has to teach World History.

You and Marcy go to your pediatrician. Dr. O'Hara is an extremely taciturn man who sometimes goes whole appointments without speaking, and you're really hoping this will be one of those appointments. But after five minutes of his silently examining you, you break down and confess that you lost your virginity the day before and you're really worried and scared that maybe you're hemorrhaging internally.

Dr. O'Hara blinks and for a moment you think he's not going to say anything, but what he does say is that you appear to have appendicitis and he wants Marcy to drive you straight over to the hospital, which Marcy does. The hospital admits you and rushes you right up to surgery while Marcy calls your parents at work and bursts into tears and your parents tell her, over and over, how proud they are of both of you, how grown up and responsible you were, how you two did just the right thing.

The night you have your appendix out is pretty awful, but by the next afternoon, you're feeling much better. Your parents stay with you during the day and when they leave, Marcy comes to visit. It's snowing so hard out that the nurses look the other way and let her sleep in the empty bed in your room, and even bring her a supper tray. Mr. Eagleton has sent you three dozen yellow roses (you told your parents they were from the golf team) and Marcy gives you a pair of earrings and the nurses must be bored because they keep stopping by your room to talk, and outside your window the hospital grounds are draped in a wedding gown of new-fallen snow. You have never felt so happy or so loved.

You and Mr. Eagleton are becoming regulars at the Starlite Motel. The first time you stayed in the car while Mr. Eagleton checked in, but now you go in with him to see what name he uses when he signs the register. He always chooses characters from your favorite novels: Mr. and Mrs. Gatsby, Mr. and Mrs. Caulfield, Mr. and Mrs. Finch, Mr. and Mrs. Twist. It seems very romantic to you even though you would never change your name, and certainly not to Eagleton.

The woman behind the counter seems to like Mr. and Mrs. Butler best. "Ah, the Rhett Butlers," she says every time. "Welcome back."

She is a large motherly woman who looks a lot like Mrs. Harrison, the woman who drives the Children's Bookmobile. She always has the TV on and always on a channel showing *Wheel of Fortune*. She's unbelievably good—you once saw her guess *Apocalypse Now* just from the letter *C*.

This woman makes you feel a lot better. Nothing bad can happen to you here.

Mr. Eagleton tells you that he's going to give you a B in history, so that no one will suspect anything.

"But I'm already getting an A," you say. "It's probably *more* suspicious if I get a B for A work."

"Leave it to me," Mr. Eagleton says, which you find beyond annoying.

At least it's American History and not English, because you really couldn't have taken that.

You will graduate eleventh in your class, nudged out of the top ten by Pricilla Todd, an annoying girl with a waterfall of red hair who takes almost exclusively typing classes. Will you think about the B in history bitterly for many years? You better believe it.

Mr. Eagleton is always going on about how this has to be secret—no texts, no e-mails—and how you can't tell anybody. And you don't tell anybody, not one single person except Marcy, and Marcy is almost less like a person and more like your frontal lobe, so that doesn't really count. And then Mr. Eagleton tells you that *he* told Mr. Poole, who is not only a person but also your geography teacher.

"What did he *say*?" you ask.

"He said that you were gorgeous," Mr. Eagleton tells you, "and also that you seem ten years older than all the other girls."

The gorgeous part is really nice but you're not so sure about the ten years older part.

"And he said that in his experience, teenage girls can't fuck or suck at all," Mr. Eagleton adds.

"What experience is that?" you ask.

"I don't know," Mr. Eagleton says, but his eyes slide away.

You are beginning to realize that although it's always hilarious to hear teachers call each other by their first names and even more hilarious to hear them making weekend plans, often they say things to each other that aren't hilarious at all.

Mr. Eagleton shows you a porn film—it turns out he has a fairly extensive collection. You are young enough to still have your parents always in the back of your mind, and you are heartbroken to think that your mother lives in a world where such films exist.

Which is not to say that you don't enjoy it. You only wish Marcy were there to watch it with you, because that would make it real. That's the problem with Mr. Eagleton—he's unreal. The part of your life that contains him is too sealed off, like the last slice of cake under one of those glass domes.

· ·

Marcy tells her parents that she's sleeping at your house so she can stay out past her curfew or even all night. She's going over to Jeff Lippencott's house, and his parents are out of town.

You agree, of course you do—think of all the times Marcy has covered for you. You sit in the TV room, wearing sweats and your glasses and eating cold Pop-Tarts. You would only ever wish the very best for Marcy, but it is hard to think of her at Jeff Lippencott's, maybe lying in his parents' bed, leading a real life.

Marcy knocks on the window a little after eleven. You open it and she steps over the window ledge, shaking little diamonds of cold rain from her hair, and says, "Oh, my God, he's such an asshole! He spent the whole time doing keg stands with his friends and I didn't know anyone and wound up helping his little sister weave potholders."

This should make you feel lots better. It should make you happy to be you again. But it doesn't.

You and Mr. Eagleton go away for the weekend and in the process you learn many life lessons, although it will take some time for them to sink in. You learn that if you tell your parents you're going to a model United Nations weekend, it's so boring they won't question it. You learn that bed-and-breakfasts have the same furniture as hotel rooms, only arranged as inconveniently as possible. You learn that all those funny and interesting lectures Mr. Eagleton gave in class are not as funny or interesting the second time, and not with you as a captive audience. You learn that sometimes the very best part of going away for a weekend with a man is planning which clothes to wear.

When you get back Sunday night, Marcy calls and asks if it

was incredibly romantic and you say yes because you don't have the heart to tell her that if you'd wanted to listen to boring shit about supply-side economics, you could have just stayed home.

Geography is one of your more effortless subjects, which is just as well because Mr. Poole is a fairly effortless teacher. Anyway, it's not biology, where you have to be hypervigilant lest some confusing fact escape you, and you have time to observe Mr. Poole as he sits at his desk, grading papers. The top of his head is bald and freckled and the skin looks thick and sort of slimy, like a toadstool or an oyster, and you wonder who the girl was, the one who was no good at sucking or fucking, and how she could bring herself to even try either one with Mr. Poole, and you hope wherever she is, she's happy now and that she hardly ever thinks about it—

Right about this time, Mr. Poole looks up and meets your gaze over the top of his bifocals and you realize with a Klondike-cold sort of clarity that Mr. Poole has these same thoughts about you, only sort of the opposite.

It should be an extremely awkward moment, but it's not, and after a second, you bow your head back over your textbook, thinking how strange it is that in a school of three thousand students and staff, you and Mr. Poole should be the two who understand each other perfectly.

These are your top five concerns at the moment:

1. College applications
2. Biology midterm

3. AP English exam
4. Money for a new phone
5. Summer internship

Mr. Eagleton is probably in the top ten somewhere, though definitely lower than the golf team. He's more like a club, not even a sport, and you think about him as much as you think about chess club, if you were the sort of person who belonged to chess club.

Apparently Mr. Eagleton feels a little differently. "I dream about being married to you," he says.

"But I'm going to college," you say.

And whatever he was hoping you'd say, it wasn't that.

Mr. Eagleton likes to talk about motorcycles, cars, football, jazz, and hiking, none of which are interesting to hear about, especially jazz. In fact, if you made a Venn diagram (you're learning about them in algebra) of your interests and Mr. Eagleton's interests, the overlapping part would be really tiny, hardly big enough to write the word *sex* in.

Mr. Eagleton still won't send texts or e-mails (he's says they're like Styrofoam and never go away) but he writes you letters. Long, passionate, sexually explicit letters—but in the end, sort of repetitive. At first you read them all thoroughly, conscientiously, but later you just glance through them, the way you look at the vocab right before a biology quiz. You fold them and, one by one, shove them all in a drawer in your desk.

It doesn't occur to you that you have a weapon of mass destruction in your desk drawer. You parents would never snoop, and even if they did, they probably wouldn't believe it. The worst that would happen is that your mother would bake brownies in the repressive way she did after she found used condoms in the yard once. All those years of straight A's and National Honor Society and Junior Achievement have an unexpected benefit: any misdeed can now be cloaked by the skirts of your goody-goody reputation. You didn't plan it that way, but you would have if you'd thought of it.

The closest you ever come to being discovered is one night at dinner, when your father says mildly, "What's up with your grades? You haven't gotten higher than a B in history all year."

In addition to marriage and the porn film, Mr. Eagleton has other ideas. One of them is anal sex. You think he's joking when he first mentions it, but it turns out that the joke is on you.

You know Mr. Eagleton has an ex-wife, although he never talks about her, and you know he has ex-girlfriends, and you're pretty sure he has ex-teenage-girlfriends, students like you. But you don't know this for certain until one day when you're lying in bed together—you're tracing cracks in the ceiling with your eyes—and he says, "I wish I could take a picture of you right now."

"You already have a picture of me," you say, and he does. It's one Marcy took of you. It took nearly two hours to get your hair to look like that.

"A picture of the way you look right now," he says.

You sit up. "I'm not going to let you take a picture of me naked."

He shrugs. "It's a good thing Poole and I have this deal to clean out each other's desks if either of us dies unexpectedly. Because there are other pictures that could get me in trouble, too."

What is it with people and their desk drawers? Mr. Eagleton is looking at you with a falsely modest look. You realize he wants you to burn with jealousy, but you only wish you could ask for your picture back.

One day at the Starlite, Mr. Eagleton signs the register "Mr. and Mrs. Baggins." This is disappointing on a lot of levels, not the least of which is that you don't even like Tolkien.

Even the woman behind the counter seems let down. She moves her cough drop from one side of her mouth to the other before she hands over the key. "There you go, Rhett," she says to Mr. Eagleton.

Then she glances at the TV and says, "Gingerbread House."

Mr. Eagleton is already holding the door of the office open. "Are you coming?" he says.

"In a minute," you say. You are looking at the TV, too. You have never wanted to watch *Wheel of Fortune* so much in your whole entire life.

You tell Marcy about the Mr. and Mrs. Baggins thing and she says, "Oh, *yuck*." (She said that about the anal sex, too, only less vehemently.)

"I know," you say. And the thing is: you do know. There's really that little to say about it.

You tell Mr. Eagleton you can't stay after school anymore. You say you can't go out in the evenings. You say your parents are suspicious. You say you're grounded for drinking vodka in Marcy's basement. You say that you lost your phone and haven't replaced it. You tell him your computer crashed. You tell him you have PMS.

To all of these, Mr. Eagleton says, "Don't you fucking lie to me."

Well, he is a teacher, after all. He's the one who told you that when you call in sick someplace, you shouldn't cough. Don't overdo it, he said.

If only Mr. Eagleton were a guy your age. Then you could have Marcy tell him you don't want to see him anymore and he would go out with all his friends and drink beer behind the bleachers until he threw up and that would be the end of it.

But because he's your teacher, you have to see him for fifty minutes every day and even though you enter class with your books clutched to your chest and your eyes downcast like a nun (isn't it nuns who do that?), occasionally you have to look up and when you do, Mr. Eagleton is always looking right back at you with his eyes burning like chili peppers. And when he lectures and walks around the classroom, sometimes he stops by your desk and you can tell that he wants to reach out and touch you, and your heart beats very fast until he moves on. Your essays come back with big red Cs on them—once scrawled so hard it left a hole in the paper.

He stands by the door these days when he dismisses class—something he never used to do—and you have to walk right past him and you can tell from his breath that maybe he's been drinking beer behind the bleachers after all.

The phone rings all the time and then the caller hangs up when your parents answer. For three straight days, you get no mail at all and your father calls the post office and complains. It appears your trash has been gone through. One night during dinner, your mother pauses with her fork midair and says, "Do I hear that motorcycle again?" During golf, another player says, "Isn't that Mr. Eagleton in front of the clubhouse?" causing you to three-putt the very last hole of the season. (Thanks a lot.) Someone leaves a "Baketacular" gift basket on your porch and your father thinks it's from his office and eats all the scones.

"Mr. Eagleton needs to grow up," says Marcy, who has come over to eat the blueberry muffins.

This confirms something you have long suspected: Marcy—Marcy, who says things like, "I never knew you weren't supposed to put tin foil in the microwave"—is actually more mature than Mr. Eagleton.

Thank heaven you leave for college as soon as school is out. You have a summer internship at an art museum in Virginia. Mr. Eagleton doesn't know this.

On the day you leave, the neighbors turn out to see you off, but all you can think of is how horrible it would be if Mr. Eagleton rode his motorcycle by right now and saw the car sitting in the driveway, packed with so many cartons and suitcases that your father can't put the front seat back. (He's already in the car and looks like a cockroach driving a matchbox.)

You are so busy worrying about this that you forget your and Marcy's ironclad rule not to go near Mr. Finnerty after he's been watching baseball and drinking six-packs. You let him hug you good-bye along with everyone else and Mr. Finnerty kisses you on the mouth and gives your ass a little squeeze. Everyone looks mortified except Marcy, who looks delighted, and your mother, who is staring off into the middle distance. You are so sure she's going to go inside and bake brownies as soon as you leave.

You climb into the car next to your father, and you should be happy but the realization that you won't see Marcy later to discuss Mr. Finnerty is like an oil slick on your heart, black and treacherous. You are much sadder about this than you will be years later when you hear that Mr. Eagleton's motorcycle hit a real oil slick and spun into a tree.

When that happens, you won't feel a thing.

GRENDEL'S MOTHER

Dr. Andy beamed up at Maya from between the stirrups and said, "Everything looks great!"

Maya wasn't sure whether this was a medical observation or a compliment of some kind, so she only said, "Mmmm," diplomatically. She was twelve weeks pregnant.

Dr. Andy finished the exam and stood up. "You're doing so well!" he said. He was only in his late twenties, very sincere, and relentlessly cheerful.

His upbeat attitude combined with the fact that everyone called him Dr. Andy instead of Dr. Lewiston reminded Maya of a preschool teacher. She liked this about him. She literally could not picture him giving her bad news, and because she could not imagine it, she felt it wouldn't happen. (But Maya's previous doctor, who'd retired last year, had always had her leave her underwear on until just before the exam, when he'd remove it. He said this was so Maya would feel more comfortable, but she'd always suspected he just liked slipping off girls' panties. So she hadn't been what you might call especially fortunate in ob-gyn choices.)

Now Dr. Andy said to his nurse, "You can call in her partner for the ultrasound."

The nurse was an older, capable-looking woman, and Maya

assumed she actually ran the whole practice, and might even be Dr. Andy's mother. The nurse left the exam room and returned with Rhodes a moment later.

Dr. Andy shook his hand. "So nice to meet Maya's partner!"

"We're married," Maya said from the exam table.

"Maya's husband then," Dr. Andy said heartily.

"We don't have rings anymore," Rhodes said, "because Maya turned out to be allergic to hers and had to have the fire department cut it off the day after the wedding, and I left mine on the nightstand at an old girlfriend's house."

Dr. Andy laughed, but Maya knew he laughed at everything. "That's a joke about the old girlfriend," she said for the nurse's benefit. "His ring actually fell off in the Pacific Ocean on our honeymoon."

"Luckily we're not big believers in foreshadowing," Rhodes said. "Although you'll notice we haven't replaced them. We're sort of waiting to see how things pan out."

Maya sighed. There were reasons—good ones—that she hadn't brought Rhodes with her before.

The nurse put a dollop of astoundingly cold gel on Maya's stomach and smeared it around. Then Dr. Andy ran the ultrasound probe over the gel, and after a moment, he turned the screen of the ultrasound machine so they all could see it.

Maya had friends whose doctors had 3-D color ultrasound machines, but evidently Dr. Andy was still saving up for one of those. The image on the screen was old-fashioned and grainy, black and white. But there was her baby, or fetus, she supposed, floating in the darkness.

"The baby's back is to us," Dr. Andy explained. "You can see the nice straight spine and the head, and there is the heart beating."

She and Rhodes both stared at that little fluttering of heartbeat. It reminded Maya of a butterfly.

Rhodes squeezed her hand. "Who'd have thought a spontaneous moment on my parents' couch after a bottle of tequila would lead to this?"

Dr. Andy laughed. Maya glanced at the nurse and found her frowning back harshly. "He's an acquired taste," Maya said.

It wasn't true, what Rhodes said about the conception of their baby. Or rather, the spontaneous part wasn't true, because they'd been trying to get pregnant for six months. Unfortunately the couch and the tequila were accurate.

After the doctor's appointment, they drove over to Rhodes's parents' house to tell them the news, now that Maya was officially past the first trimester.

"Oh, my God!" Rhodes's mother, Hazelene, shrieked. "I'm so happy! I'm happier than you are!"

Rhodes's father opened a bottle of champagne, and they all sat in the living room (Maya even sat on the couch!) and drank it. Although instead of champagne Maya had milk, which turned out to be the only nonalcoholic, decaffeinated beverage in the house.

"Have you thought about names?" Hazelene asked. She did seem excited, and kept bouncing up and down slightly on her chair cushion.

"What names do you like, Mom?" Rhodes asked. "And whatever you answer, we'll say 'Not that.'"

"I've always liked Thor for a boy," Hazelene said. "And Grendel for a girl."

"That so proves my point," Rhodes said.

Just then Magellan, Rhodes's eighteen-year-old sister, and her boyfriend, Toby, arrived.

Hazelene popped out of her chair like a jack-in-the-box. "Maya and Rhodes are going to have a baby!"

Magellan looked at Maya for confirmation, as though Hazelene said this sort of thing all the time, whether it was true or not. Maya nodded.

"Cool," said Magellan. She was still stocky, with none of Rhodes's tall skinny grace. "Congratulations."

Toby didn't say anything, but he never said anything. He wore his iPod constantly, the little white buds tucked into his ears every single second Maya had ever been in his presence. He was a tall scrawny boy with long blond hair that he constantly flicked out of his eyes by jerking his head slightly.

He accepted the glass of champagne Rhodes's father handed him, and raised it when they all made a toast.

"Does he even know what he's drinking to?" Rhodes asked Magellan, and she gave an impatient nod, like Rhodes was an idiot for asking.

Toby and Magellan seemed to Maya not so much a couple as animal and trainer, Toby being the animal. Like Clever Hans and his owner, or Curious George and the Man with the Yellow Hat, although Toby was not as interesting (or probably as intelligent) as Curious George.

Rhodes's parents never objected to Toby's constant iPod-wearing, or the fact that he always asked (through Magellan) what they were having before he agreed to stay for dinner. Maya didn't know whether they accepted this antisocial behavior because they thought Toby was probably the best that Magellan could do, or because they had failed to notice it. They could be kind of clueless sometimes.

"To Grendel!" Hazelene cried out happily, raising her glass again. Maya thought maybe so much champagne before dinner was not a good idea.

"Or Thor," added Rhodes's father.

Toby flicked his bangs out his eyes, and Magellan said, "Why are we talking about *Beowulf*?"

Yes, Maya had voluntarily married into this family, had in fact chosen one of its members to father her child, was willingly about to partake of its gene pool. (It seemed to Maya that each of those phrases should be followed by an exclamation point— family! child! gene pool!) She knew Rhodes would look at this from an evolutionary perspective, and say that Maya was seeking some trait that neither she nor her family possessed. But most of the time Maya just thought she had taken complete leave of her senses.

Hazelene phoned a few days later and said, "Hello, Maya, dear. Are you and Grendel busy this morning?"

Everyone was calling Maya's unborn baby Grendel now. Maya tried very hard to believe this was an in utero name only, and that the baby would grow up being called by whatever name she and Rhodes decided to give it, but she had some doubts. She knew early nicknames could stick.

"No, I'm not doing anything right now," Maya said. (She worked at the library only two days a week.) She understood, and was pleased, that Hazelene was tremendously excited about her first grandchild, but she refused to act as though Grendel had a separate social life until Grendel actually did.

"I was wondering if you might stop by," Hazelene said. "It seems that Magellan and Toby have had a small misunderstanding—"

"He *broke up* with me," Magellan said forcefully in the background.

"And we're in a bit of a crisis and could use your wisdom," Hazelene finished.

"Okay, I'll be right over," Maya said.

She was actually flattered to have been invited. She felt like a head of state summoned to an international summit on terrorism. Although when she arrived at Rhodes's parents' house half an hour later, she found it somewhat disappointing as international summits go. It consisted solely of Magellan slumped at the kitchen table, staring morosely into a bowl of raisin bran while Hazelene sat across from her, reading the newspaper and wondering aloud why the farmers' market had been moved from Wednesday to Tuesday.

Maya pulled up a chair and opened the bottle of orange juice she'd brought with her. "So what happened? Why did you break up?" she asked in an attempt to get things started.

A small beat of silence followed, during which Maya wondered if the answer to that question was something Hazelene was prepared to hear. What if Magellan started talking about blow jobs?

But all Magellan did was push her cereal bowl away and cover her face with her hands. "I don't know!" she said hoarsely. "He won't tell me! All he did is say it's over and now he won't answer his phone or anything!"

"I'm sure there was a reason, dear," Hazelene said gently.

Maya said nothing at all because, quite unexpectedly, her heart had constricted with sympathy to the point where speech was impossible.

Because, really, was there any breakup more painful than an unexplained one? Certainly, Hazelene was right and there was a reason, but unless Toby chose to tell Magellan, she would never know what it was. It could be that Toby had started seeing some other girl. It could be that Toby had been seeing some other girl for the whole time he had been seeing Magellan. It could be that Toby had met some girl so bewitching, so superior to Magellan in every way, that just the knowledge of her existence made Toby not want to be with Magellan anymore. It could be that Toby was gay, or bisexual, or had decided to become a priest. It could be that his parents disapproved of Magellan. It could be that his *friends* disapproved of Magellan. It could be some personal detail about Magellan, like Toby thought she wasn't smart enough or social enough or funny enough. It could be, hideously, some personal *physical* detail about Magellan, like that he thought her stomach was wobbly or she didn't clean her fingernails well or her hair smelled funny. It could be something Magellan had said, which Toby had taken the wrong way, like her dismissing the Arctic Monkeys' talent, or a joke about iPods that didn't go over that well. It could be *anything,* and that was the most maddening part of all. And Maya knew, from personal experience, that the reason behind the breakup could become, in a way, even more anguishing than the breakup itself, if you never found out what it was. It could haunt you for months, even for years, the unknown reason, and take on a nearly mythical importance, until you forgot, or almost forgot, that the *truly* important thing was that someone you wanted to be with no longer wanted to be with you.

The next night Rhodes rubbed Maya's back as they lay in bed. The pregnancy was making it ache. Rhodes gave very good back rubs and Maya made a low appreciative sound.

"On any given day, would you rather have sex or a back rub?" Rhodes asked.

"Both," Maya said sleepily.

"What, half-and-half?" Rhodes asked. "Or is this some sort of two-man fantasy and if so, which man do I get to be?"

Before she could answer, the phone rang. Rhodes picked it up and said, "Hello?" and then he said "Ye-es" in that wary, speculative way he did when it was a telemarketer. Then he went quiet for so long that Maya thought it must not be a telemarketer, unless it was one selling something Rhodes might actually be interested in, like blue laser pointers.

Finally, he said, "Let me talk it over with Maya and I'll call you back." He hung up. "That was Magellan. She wants to move in with us for a while."

"Why?"

Rhodes began rubbing her back again. "Apparently my parents are driving her crazy about her big breakup. My mom wants them to take a pottery course together and my dad keeps, like, speaking to inanimate objects and then saying, 'Sorry, I thought that was Toby for a minute.'" Rhodes laughed, and Maya was glad he had not laughed on the phone. "Don't worry, I'll call her back in five minutes and tell her no."

"I don't mind if she stays with us," Maya said. "For a little while."

Rhodes stopped rubbing. "Really?"

"Really," Maya said.

"Why?"

"I feel bad for her," Maya said. But the truth was not as simple as that. The truth was that Brad Redington had broken up with Maya the day after senior prom, after dating her for six months, and never given her a single reason for the breakup, and apparently Maya was such a rigid, narrow person that she could have sympathy for someone only if she had endured an almost identical misfortune.

"Well, okay," Rhodes said.

He picked up the phone and dialed. Magellan must have answered because Rhodes said immediately, "Okay, as long as you move out before the baby's born and hopefully a whole lot sooner."

Maya had failed to foresee certain things, or, to be honest, forgotten all about them, when she agreed to let Magellan come live with them. She had forgotten that they'd given the bed in the spare room to the Salvation Army to make room for the baby furniture, which meant Magellan would have to sleep on the living room couch. Magellan didn't object to this, but she seemed to consider the living room her personal domain and within hours of her arrival, it looked like a family of vagrants (a very modern family with lots of electronics) had moved in with all their earthly goods.

Maya had also forgotten how messy teenagers were, how they left their clothes on the floor, and their towels on the chairs, and their hairs in the sink, and their half-filled coffee cups and Diet Coke cans on every possible surface. And Magellan seemed to eat trail mix more or less constantly, leaving grit on the floor to crunch under Maya's bare feet.

Maya had forgotten that it was the first week of summer vacation, and Magellan didn't have a summer job (or very much desire to get one, apparently) so she was around the house all the time.

And since Maya worked at home three days a week, that meant a lot of together time. Which led to *another* thing Maya had forgotten, namely that she didn't really like Magellan very much.

She had not remembered that Magellan, for the most part, was silent, and sullen, and lazy, or the fact that when she did talk, her stories had no discernible end, and just trailed off aimlessly, driving Maya berserk. And she had forgotten that Magellan judged her all the time. When Maya brought in groceries, Magellan looked them over skeptically but did not offer to help unpack. If Maya took a nap in the afternoon, Magellan raised her eyebrows—Magellan, who did nothing but sit on the couch and stare at the TV all day! Magellan watched the way Maya moved and ate and dressed and showered and kept her house and talked to Rhodes, and she had opinions on it all, Maya knew, because Maya remembered being a teenager; oh, that, Maya remembered.

By the fourth night of Magellan's stay, Maya and Rhodes had taken to going to bed, or at least to their bedroom, at eight o'clock. "She's going to think we're such losers," Maya said.

"Then go out and talk to her if you don't want her to think that," Rhodes said. He was sitting in bed with his laptop. Suddenly he banged the keyboard. "*And* she's been using my laptop to download music from illegal websites, and now I have a webserver using our bandwidth to serve up Japanese cartoon porn."

Maya went to the bathroom to brush her teeth. Nowhere in the house was Magellan's presence more obvious. Every inch of available countertop in the bathroom was now covered with miniature bottles of cosmetics and perfumes and lotions. Maya was both fascinated and depressed by this collection. How many trips to the store would it have taken to accumulate all these free samples? And yet Magellan didn't realize that her looks were not the problem. Her looks were actually fine, or potentially fine, if she had the personality to make you forget them. All these little tubes of things weren't the answer. For the first time, Maya hoped that Grendel would be a boy. Girls were nothing but heartbreak.

Maya craved the chicken tenders from Bennigan's, and so she and Rhodes began to go there for dinner once or twice a week. It was also a good way to escape Magellan, who said she didn't want to be seen there with them, no offense.

Tonight they were waiting to be seated and a woman in front of them in line turned around and said, "Rhodes?"

Maya had no idea who this woman was, but obviously Rhodes did, because he completely lost the thread of something he was saying about grid engines and stared at her.

The woman smiled and touched the arm of the man next to her, who also turned around. "This is my husband, Jeff," she said. "Jeff, this is Rhodes Hollenbeck, and . . ."

"This is my wife, Maya," Rhodes said. "She's pregnant."

"That's not why we got married, though," Maya added. She meant it sardonically, but Jeff just nodded and said, "Oh, right."

"This is Kimmy Brinkman," Rhodes finally said, and Maya could only think *Kimmy Brinkman!* Only not so much the words as a general kind of thrilled eagerness, the way she might feel if someone told her she had won a trip to the Caribbean.

Just then the hostess came up and said, "Table for four?"

Kimmy Brinkman said, "Sure, that would be great," and they all went and sat in a booth together and the whole time Maya kept thinking *Kimmy Brinkman!* in the same excited way.

This was Kimmy Brinkman! This woman with the short blond hair and the small nose and the blue cardigan. This was Kimmy

Brinkman, for whom Rhodes had pined all of his junior year of high school while she dated a senior. Kimmy Brinkman, who had finally consented to date Rhodes when the senior went to college. Kimmy Brinkman, to whom Rhodes had lost his virginity in the storage space next to his parents' kitchen while Hazelene chalked the shopping list on the blackboard ten yards away. Kimmy Brinkman, who had performed oral sex on Rhodes in the special education playground late at night (the only place they could think to go where no one would look for them). Kimmy Brinkman, who had gone on summer vacation with Rhodes's family and not been allowed to share a bedroom with Rhodes. Kimmy Brinkman, who had taken Rhodes on summer vacation with *her* family and they *had* been allowed to share a bedroom, but they hadn't had sex because Rhodes had been fearful of Kimmy's father storming the room in his underwear with a shotgun, even though her father was apparently very mild-mannered.

Oh, the things Maya knew about Kimmy Brinkman, and here she was having dinner with her! It seemed as improbable as having dinner with Abraham Lincoln or Winston Churchill. Well, maybe a bit more probable, given that Kimmy was a) alive and b) living in the next town over, where she was a partner in a dermatology practice and her husband, Jeff, owned a dog-grooming business.

Unfortunately, there wasn't any way, or at least any way Maya could see, to discuss the things she knew about Kimmy Brinkman. So instead they had to talk about Maya's due date, and whether February is a good or bad time to have a birthday, and why Rhodes hadn't gone to his high school reunion, and how the economic crisis was affecting the dog-grooming industry. Eventually, Maya stopped thinking *Kimmy Brinkman!* every few seconds and started thinking about chicken tenders in the same way, which was what she'd been doing in the first place.

In the car on the way home, she said, "I can't believe I finally met Kimmy Brinkman."

"And she was awful!" Rhodes said with unexpected heat.

"Really?" Maya said. "I didn't think so. She told me I should do the exact same thing to my skin every single night."

"You don't understand," Rhodes said. "I used to look at her in Advanced Algebra and some days I thought the school could literally collapse and kill us and I would die happy because Kimmy Brinkman loved me. And now she's a dermatologist married to a dog groomer and she only reads books from Oprah's Book Club!"

Maya wanted to argue that being a dermatologist was a totally respectable occupation, but she had to agree with him about the dog groomer and certainly about Oprah's Book Club. So instead she said mildly, "You just drove past our turn."

"Sorry," Rhodes said, checking the mirror and getting ready to do a U-turn. "I just can't get over how awful she is."

Maya thought perhaps she should be jealous that Rhodes had once felt that way about Kimmy Brinkman, because she was pretty sure he'd never felt that way about her, but she wasn't. She also thought that maybe it would have been nice to meet Kimmy Brinkman when she, Maya, wasn't wearing pants that looked an inch too short because of her expanding stomach, but she didn't really mind about that either. Mainly she just thought that she and Rhodes were different. That Rhodes would, apparently, still like to feel the way he had in high school, and Maya couldn't think of anything worse.

· ·

Maya drove Magellan over to Rhodes's parents' house so she could collect a few things. (Just a *few*, Rhodes emphasized before they left.) And while Magellan was busy up in her room, Hazelene said, "I have something to show you," and led Maya to her bedroom.

Hazelene took a fabric hatbox off the top shelf of her closet. "I didn't save very many baby things," she said. "But I thought I'd show you what I have."

She dumped the contents of the hatbox unceremoniously on the bed and started picking through them.

"This is a little sweater and cap that my mother knitted and all of my babies wore home from the hospital," she said, smoothing out a tiny white cardigan and matching hat with tassels. "Though only Rhodes's head was small enough to wear the cap."

This sounded vaguely insulting toward Rhodes, like maybe he was less intelligent than the rest of his family. But Maya liked the little sweater and cap. "I'd love to have those," she said.

"And here are two maternity tops," Hazelene said, shaking them both out and spreading them on the bed. "I can't really remember why I saved these two. They must look ugly by today's standards."

They did indeed. One was especially hideous, bright green with big white polka dots. The other was a beige cotton tunic with colorful embroidery around the neckline, and was sort of okay, or would be if Maya were Swedish and wore flowers in her hair.

"Oh, they're not ugly," Maya said. "Now they're considered retro or vintage."

She could tell by Hazelene's expression that neither of those words meant anything and she might as well have said "corbomite" and "horta." Although those were *Star Trek* terms and

Hazelene may easily have understood them because Rhodes had
been a big fan of *Star Trek* as a preteen and once in an attempt at
mother-son bonding, he and Hazelene had gone to a convention
in Chicago . . . Maya shook her head. It really didn't bear thinking about.

Instead she looked at the other items that had fallen out of
the hatbox. There were some yellowed envelopes that Maya
assumed contained copies of birth announcements, and a few
silver spoons, and several tiny vinyl hospital identification bracelets. Maya picked one of the bracelets up and smoothed it out to
see if it was Rhodes's. But the name on the bracelet read *Pascal
Livingston Hollenbeck.*

Maya looked at Hazelene. "You had a baby named Pascal?"

"Is that his bracelet?" Hazelene asked. She took it from Maya
gently. "Yes, I did, but he died when he was just a day old. They
said he had a bacterial infection."

"Oh, Hazelene," Maya breathed. "How—how unbearable."

"It was not an easy time," Hazelene sounded matter-of-fact.
"But a year later we had Rhodes and then things were okay."

"I've never seen his grave," Maya said softly. She had been to
the cemetery with Rhodes's family when his grandmother died.

"He's buried in Delaware, where we lived then," Hazelene
said. "I've never been back to see his grave actually. I hope sometimes that they take good care of it, but they do, generally, at
cemeteries, keep all the graves tidy, don't you think?"

"Oh, yes," Maya said automatically.

She was often surprised by information, things other people
seemed to know. She never knew until last month that you had
to have your boiler serviced, and yet virtually every other person
who owned a house must know that. And it was only this year,
during a conversation about jet lag, that she learned the Earth

spun from west to east. She had known, of course, that the Earth rotated, but she had never wondered—never considered! never thought about it!—which direction. And she had not known until now, this very minute, that you could carry a baby for nine months, give birth to it, watch him die, leave his body buried in a distant state, and hope that strangers tended its grave—that you could do all that and not stagger around for the rest of your life with a gaping wound in your middle. You could live through that and thirty years later you could be a functional, basically cheerful person anticipating the birth of your first grandchild. This knowledge swept through Maya with such force that she had to close her eyes for a second.

When she opened her eyes, she knew she ought to hug Hazelene, but curiously, Hazelene did not seem to need hugging, and was busy stuffing everything back into the hatbox.

"Wait," Maya said. "I want the maternity tops, too." She vowed that she would wear them both, even the one with polka dots.

The next time they went to Bennigan's, as the hostess led them to a table, they turned a corner and there, sitting in a booth, was Dr. Andy.

He glanced up. "Why, Maya, hello."

Apparently there was a whole social life to be had at Bennigan's and Maya had never been aware of it. She wished she still wasn't aware of it. She thought maybe Magellan was right about not wanting to come here.

Maya hoped it would not turn out that Dr. Andy was eating alone. She peered into the other side of the booth, and was happy to see a nice-looking Hispanic woman sitting opposite him.

"Hi, Dr. Andy," Maya said. "You remember my husband, Rhodes."

"Yes, of course," Dr. Andy said. "And this is . . . Patricia."

Patricia smiled at them, somewhat wanly it seemed to Maya, and Rhodes said, "I see you have an iPhone. What's your opinion on their firmware?"

But Maya was thinking about the way Dr. Andy had introduced Patricia. Why hadn't he said *my girlfriend* or even *my friend*? Why did Patricia look so uncomfortable? Why did Dr. Andy seem subdued? Why were they both picking at an order of nachos and nursing watery margaritas? Oh God, were they breaking up—here and now? Were there any fates worse than breaking up at Bennigan's over nachos? (Yes, yes, of course there were. Think of all the Filipinos being kidnapped by Abu Sayyaf! But in a way there weren't.)

Eventually the hostess cleared her throat, and Maya and Rhodes continued on to their own table, but Maya could barely concentrate. She was thinking about how when she was trying to get pregnant, it seemed like the rest of the world was having babies with the greatest of ease, and of how, when she was younger, it seemed like everyone she knew was in long-term relationships while Maya was still sleeping with men who didn't always call her again. And how eventually, you got what you wanted—lover, husband, baby—and you still remembered that you had once felt lonely and bereft and incomplete, but you forgot that other people went on feeling that way. You forgot that some people never got what they wanted, or got it and managed to keep it only briefly. You forgot about all that love out in the world, with no place to go. It seemed to Maya that Bennigan's was full of that sad, superfluous love tonight, a dark pulsing cloud of it, pushing in on her from all sides—

"What's wrong?" Rhodes asked. He reached across the table and held her hand.

Maya blinked back tears. "Nothing," she whispered. "Just hormones."

How could she and Rhodes bring a baby into such a world? What were they thinking?

Maya got so sleepy one afternoon at the library that she actually dozed off at the Interlibrary Loan Desk with her head on her hand. Her boss told her to take the rest of the day off, so Maya went home.

She was pleased to find that Magellan had actually gone out somewhere, and she walked past the living room, unbuttoning her blouse. She intended to sleep the afternoon away.

When she opened her bedroom door, her first reaction was one of annoyance that Magellan's stuff was now in here, too— her clothes on the floor, and her flip-flops bunching up the throw rug. But then Maya realized, with something like horror, that not only was Magellan's stuff in here, but *Magellan* was, too, in the bed, under the covers, writhing around with someone.

Maya's pretty white comforter was thrown back and Toby's head appeared. Magellan was beneath him, and it was obvious that the reason they hadn't heard Maya was that they were both wearing headphones connected to Toby's iPod, which rested on Maya's own pillow, its screen flashing.

Toby tossed his head to clear his bangs, and at that moment, he saw Maya. "Oh, shit," he said distinctly. (He spoke! He spoke! Any other time, Maya would have been thrilled.)

Magellan opened her eyes then and saw Maya, too. She made an inarticulate noise, which sounded just like Maya's mother's cat last Christmas, when it ate tinsel off the tree and threw up in the coat closet.

Maya stepped back and banged the door closed. She stood on the other side of it, panting with panic, and rebuttoned her blouse crookedly. Then she hurried back out to her car and drove to Rhodes's office.

"My first question—" Rhodes began.

"Missionary," Maya answered. "Very basic from what I could see."

"I was actually wondering where he got the splitter for the iPod headphones," Rhodes said.

"Well, was your *second* question going to be what position?" Maya said, exasperated.

Rhodes leaned back in his office chair. "No, my second question is how will we know when it's safe to go home?"

Maya groaned. "I hadn't even thought of that."

In the end, they went to Starbucks for an hour and afterward drove around aimlessly for twenty minutes. Then they went home and Maya rang their own doorbell. When nobody answered, they went inside.

Magellan was gone. Not just out, but *gone.* Gone, too, were her laptop, her phone charger, her webcam, her headphones, her novels, her notebooks, her pens and pencils, her fluffy green bathrobe, her spill-proof coffee mug, her flip-flops, her reading light, her bags of trail mix and her endless cans of Diet Coke, her pop-up laundry hamper, her hair dryer, her plastic hangers, her tangle of necklaces and her dangly earrings, her bras, her underpants, her skirts, her shirts, her jeans, her socks, her baby powder, her combs, her brushes, her eye shadow, lipsticks, tampons, hand mirror, and tweezers. All vanished from the living room floor and furniture.

"I can see the couch again!" Rhodes said happily. "She's moved out!"

But Maya—though pleased to have her living room back—felt happy not for herself and Rhodes, but for Magellan. What must have it felt like to kiss Toby, to touch him, to hold him, to undress him (or watch him undress, however they did it) after thinking for so long that she would never get to do those things again? Magellan, no matter how embarrassed, must have a light heart tonight, and Maya's own heart rose in accord.

Later, when she went into the bathroom, she saw that Magellan, either through oversight or time constraints, had not taken her dozens of little sample-size bottles and tubes. Maya swept them all into a pretty cut-glass bowl and put the bowl on top of the toilet tank as a sort of alternative potpourri. She stirred the little plastic vials with a finger. She felt an inexplicable fondness for them now, and an equally inexplicable sadness that Magellan was gone.

When Maya went in for her sixteen-week checkup, Dr. Andy was wearing a blue-and-white seersucker suit and a straw boater with a blue hatband. He looked a little crazy, but also jolly and carefree, and Maya liked that, because she desperately wanted to believe that having a baby could be a jolly, carefree experience.

Dr. Andy examined Maya (she could see the top of the boater the whole time) and then had the nurse call Rhodes in for the ultrasound.

"Wow," Rhodes said when he saw Dr. Andy. "That's quite an outfit."

"Thank you," Dr. Andy said in a pleased-sounding way. Maya wondered if it was possible to offend him, and figured Rhodes would probably find a way before the baby was born.

"You and Maya are a matched set," Rhodes said, which did offend Maya. She was wearing Hazelene's green polka-dot maternity top, and if anything, it looked even worse on than it had spread out on the bed.

She and Dr. Andy regarded each other, but evidently he didn't know quite what to say either, because after a moment, he said, "Let's do the ultrasound, shall we?"

This time, they could see Grendel's profile, and watch him or her stretching and rotating, the mouth opening, closing, and swallowing. At one point Grendel kicked in the direction of the ultrasound probe, and Dr. Andy laughed. "Very responsive for this age," he said.

Was it possible to feel a vain, superior, soccer-mom kind of pride in a sixteen-week-old fetus? Yes, Maya was sorry to realize it was, and that she was indeed feeling it. She was sad when the ultrasound was over.

After the appointment, Maya and Rhodes had to wait a long time for the elevator, which was always very slow. Maya thought it was because there were mainly doctors' offices in the building, and lots of old people shuffling on and off the elevator at every floor. Rhodes waited impatiently, pressing the call button about ten times and picking petals off the dried flower arrangement on the table. He could never hold still for long.

"Does it bother you, ever," Maya said thoughtfully, "that he's so young?"

"Babies are supposed to be young," Rhodes said.

"Not Grendel." Maya was patient. "Dr. Andy."

"Oh." Rhodes considered. "No, not really," he said at last. "He seems to know what he's doing, and you and I know what we're doing, so I think we'll be okay."

Maya wished then that the elevator would take even longer to arrive than it normally did because she wanted to savor this moment. She knew that lots of couples achieved this before they were married, let alone before they were expecting their first child, and she also knew that many couples experienced this as a continuous state and not a random occurrence, but she didn't really care. She and Rhodes, for once, felt exactly the same way.

ANDORRA

Sadie's lover Marcus called her every Thursday from Chicago as he drove to and from marriage counseling. (His wife drove separately, it goes without saying.) The end result of this was that it felt like the three of them were in counseling together, but Sadie sort of liked that.

The reason Marcus had to go to marriage counseling was that three months ago, his wife had intercepted an e-mail from Sadie. Which meant, among other things, that Marcus had to agree to go to marriage counseling and promise never to speak to Sadie again, to banish her to the Ulan Bator of his heart, while in reality Sadie remained as central as Starbucks. Sadie liked that, too.

Sadie was thirty-six. She had two little boys named Rufus and Leo, aged six and four, and a fifty-year-old husband named Roderick who worked for the Council on Foreign Relations, and a big house in Washington, D.C., and a minivan full of dog hair. The fact that she had all this and a long-distance lover seemed to her like a sign of strength and character; not many people could manage it.

Of course, Sadie had help. She had a Filipino housekeeper named Nelda. When Sadie interviewed her two years ago, Nelda had said, "I'm slow."

"I don't mind slow," Sadie had said, impressed by Nelda's candor. "I think IQ is . . . overrated." (The pause was while she looked for a simpler word for *overrated.*)

"Not slow like that," Nelda said, blinking behind her thick glasses. "Slow like not fast."

Nelda was indeed slow, and she had a disconcerting habit of going into a trance when asked questions, and it turned out that she was allergic to nearly all cleaning products. She also had a large, troubled family, many of whom came to work with her (some just hung out and made helpful suggestions, but some actually cleaned, so the house looked okay), and Sadie didn't fire her because she had a vague idea that having so many people around the house gave her children a sense of family and community that might otherwise be lacking.

This was how Sadie's life ticked along, not like a finely tuned engine, but like some other thing that ticks: noisy pipes, or a bomb.

Marcus's wife said in counseling that she wanted to spend more time with him.

"She said that the only thing we ever do together is that one of us holds the dog still while the other one puts that antiflea stuff on his neck," Marcus told Sadie afterward.

"Roderick and I do that sometimes," Sadie said thoughtfully. "It's nice."

· ·

Sadie had met Marcus a year ago when she sat next to him on a flight from Washington to Chicago. She was going to visit her parents in Wisconsin. He had asked her to name a small republic located in the Pyrenees Mountains on the French-Spanish border. (He was doing a crossword puzzle.)

It was ironic that he should ask her that because when she first started dating Roderick, her parents had offered to *pay* for her to take a geography course so she and Roderick would have something to talk about. Which was in itself ironic because Sadie had been twenty-four at the time and didn't have any trouble getting men to talk to her, Roderick included.

So instead of telling Marcus the answer (she didn't know it, anyway), Sadie told him the story of her parents' offer, and by the time the plane was over Ohio, he was already in love with her, or so he said later. And Sadie gave all the credit to the story about the geography lessons. It was everything a story should be, she felt. She was proud of it. Not everyone has a story that good.

Sadie and Roderick had to go to a dinner party at the Finnish embassy. Sadie said she hated dinner parties and Roderick said they weren't so bad if you got plastered as fast as possible. Sadie still thought the best part was probably picking out what to wear—a pink wool wraparound dress, which was new and came unwrapped if she made the slightest movement. Sadie discovered this when she walked downstairs but Nelda was already there with five or six relatives to babysit. So Sadie just rewrapped her dress and asked Nelda if she could leave one of her nieces in charge of the boys and come pick them up at ten o'clock. They gave her the address, and off she and Roderick went in a taxi.

At the dinner Sadie sat between a man who told her that he

was a world expert on the pistachio and another man who told her that he collected Early American documents as a hobby. Sadie concentrated on cutting her reindeer into very tiny pieces and drank so much red wine that her teeth turned purple. She held the thought of Marcus in her mind, like a Saint Christopher medal, or a dream catcher, or maybe just a hidden flask of whiskey in her purse—something that made survival possible.

After the dinner, they went outside to wait for Nelda to pick them up. They waited so long that Roderick said he was sober and then they waited even longer and Roderick said they could have walked home by now. Sadie said that Nelda had trouble with time and Roderick asked if she meant that Nelda had trouble with time the way some people have trouble with money. Sadie said, no, it was more that Nelda didn't believe in time, the way some people didn't believe in ESP or Bigfoot. Roderick said they really had to get some decent help, but he said that about twice a month anyway.

Finally an SUV with a bunch of Filipino people in it pulled up and Nelda rolled down the passenger window, her eyeglasses glinting opaquely in the moonlight. Sadie had a very bad moment when she was sure Nelda was going to say there wasn't room for them, but all Nelda said was "Good evening."

So Sadie squeezed in the front next to Nelda and Roderick squeezed in the back with some of Nelda's relatives. Sadie could hear him discussing the Chinese claims in the South China Sea. He sounded fairly happy. She sighed and leaned her head back.

"How was your dinner?" Nelda asked. "You enjoy yourself?"

"I sat next to a man who was an expert on *nuts*," Sadie said.

Nelda didn't say anything. Sadie closed her eyes, the passing streetlamps flashing white oblongs against her lids. Finally Nelda seemed to come to life again. She patted Sadie's hand and said, "Well, soon you be in your own bed," and Sadie thought, not for the first time, that Nelda understood her on some deep and fundamental level no one else did.

Marcus had a rule against saying bad things about their spouses. Sadie broke the rule all the time; why have an affair if not to say bad things about your spouse? So she went ahead and told Marcus that when she tried to talk to Roderick about how terrific Leo's preschool teacher was, Roderick had only told her a bunch of facts about Bosnia.

"I mean, Leo's teacher *is* from Bosnia," Sadie said, "but that wasn't what I wanted to discuss."

"What did Roderick say about Bosnia?" Marcus asked.

A small silence followed while Sadie wished that it were permissible to say bad things about your lover to your husband. But then she sighed and said, "Well, just that it's the twentieth anniversary of the siege of Sarajevo, and something about the Dayton Peace Accords."

"What's fascinating about Bosnia——" Marcus said, but Sadie had to hang up abruptly because Rufus came running into her bedroom to tell her he had a rash on his belly button.

Sadie looked at his belly button and told him it was nothing to worry about, although privately she wondered if maybe a mushroom was growing in there and resolved to give him more thorough baths. She thought that was the essence of motherhood: acting like you knew what you were talking about when you didn't. That, and looking at people's rashes. It was probably why people had affairs.

"Who wants to go to the park?" Sadie asked.

Rufus and Leo scrambled up from the sofa and, too late, Sadie realized that Nelda's assorted relatives were showing their nearly imperceptible signs of preparation as well. It would be a group outing.

They left in stages, like a military operation. First went Rufus and Leo on their little bikes with the training wheels and a couple of the sprier relatives to help them cross the streets. Next was the dog, panting and straining, the leash wrapped around the waist of one of Nelda's nephews, and the remaining relatives lending moral support. Last were Sadie and Nelda.

"Sorry," Nelda said to Sadie as she locked the front door. "I'm always last, like a caboose."

"That's okay," said Sadie, although she thought Nelda was more like an anchor than a caboose because at least a caboose went where the rest of the train went; she and Nelda might still be here when everyone else got back.

Sadie put the keys in her pocket and they began walking.

"You walk slow, you don't feel the heat," Nelda said.

It was October and they could have walked as fast as they wanted without feeling the heat, but Sadie didn't say so. Maybe it was still summer in Nelda's private world. Maybe it was *several* summers ago.

A jubilant shout and small burst of applause came from the relatives far ahead of them. Sadie knew that meant Rufus or Leo had done something praiseworthy, had pedaled up a small hill

without stopping or bumped his bike over a big crack in the sidewalk without falling over.

She was missing them grow up, she thought suddenly. They
were passing all these milestones with strangers while she talked
to Nelda and snuck away to call Marcus.

But that was foolishness. You couldn't have everything the
way you wanted all the time. You were lucky if you got it occasionally. Leo had taken his first steps at Hooters when they'd
gone there for an Australian diplomat's farewell lunch party and
Sadie had been unable to bring herself to record it in Leo's baby
book. She had given up on baby books entirely after that.

The marriage counselor wanted Marcus to do something nice for
his wife every day.

"So right away," he said to Sadie afterward, "I'm thinking:
How nice?"

"You could give her flowers," Sadie said.

"I'm not buying flowers every day," Marcus said, sounding
shocked.

"I didn't mean every day," Sadie said. "Just once, in the beginning."

"Also, I think it's sort of hilarious how much women like to
get flowers," Marcus said.

"No more hilarious than how much men like to get blow
jobs," said Sadie, who liked to get flowers herself.

"Flowers and blow jobs are *not* comparable," Marcus said,
sounding even more shocked.

"They are in how predictable it is that whoever's getting them
will like it," Sadie said. "A lot."

"They're not even in the same *category*," Marcus said.

Sadie thought they were actually very similar except that after a few really excellent blow jobs, men often fell hopelessly in love with you, whereas women knew, no matter how beautiful the flowers, that it was all for show.

Sadie was chopping celery when Nelda arrived. Sadie hardly ever cooked and Nelda gave her a big smile and squinted at her approvingly. "Ah," she said. "You making dinner for the man you love?"

"No," Sadie said. "I'm making dinner for the health minister of Togo."

Besides, Marcus was the man she loved. Or had Nelda meant Marcus? Sometimes Sadie wondered.

"Anyway," Sadie continued. "The health minister is coming here for dinner tonight at seven, so I need you, or someone, to clean the living room."

She realized as she said this, though, that Nelda was alone, a movie star without her entourage. Sadie was surprised she'd recognized her.

"Nobody come with me today," Nelda said. "They all go to vote at the embassy. Big election in the Philippines."

This seemed to happen every few weeks. And although most of the time Sadie actively suppressed the part of her brain that dealt with politics and foreign policy (she feared becoming a female version of Roderick), she wondered exactly how many elections there could be. She was just as insecure as everyone else and now suddenly she worried that all the relatives had found some other house to hang out in—someplace where the time went faster, the conversation was livelier, the atmosphere more relaxed, the hostess friendlier and funnier. Wasn't that what everyone ran around looking for, in some form or another?

"What about the living room?" she said to Nelda.

Nelda went off into a reverie, while Sadie began chopping the celery again. Finally Nelda shook her head and said no, she had to go pick up everyone else in an hour but that Sadie worried too much, she was so sweet and had such a pretty smile, no one would notice the dog hair.

Sadie and Marcus had phone sex by the bushelful.

"You don't measure phone sex by the bushel," Marcus said.

"Well, then how *do* you measure it?" Sadie asked. Sometimes she thought she'd gone crazy; other times she thought she was the only sane person left in the world.

Marcus sounded thoughtful. "Maybe by the minute."

"But I have an unlimited calling plan," Sadie said doubtfully.

"I guess it can't be measured," Marcus said.

"But it can," Sadie said. "Because you can have a lot or a little."

"Or none," Marcus said. "Like right now."

"We will," Sadie said. "In a minute. Right now I'm all distracted by phone-sex units."

"It's unique," Marcus said. "Everything else can be measured except phone sex."

Everything except love, Sadie thought. Love can't be measured in units either, unless it's by phone sex.

"Anyway," Marcus said, his voice deepening. "What are you wearing?"

"What are you wearing?" Sadie said later to Rufus when he ran through the kitchen in his underpants, and she said, "Good . . . good . . ." to Leo when he helped her mix the cake batter, and

"I'm coming," to Nelda when she said that the UPS man was there, and "I wish you were here," to her mother on the phone, and "Oh, fuck me," when the dog threw up on the carpet. She didn't say "I want you in my mouth right now," to anyone, but it occurred to her that she could get through most days with only a limited number of phrases, that it was how you said them and who you were at that moment that mattered.

Marcus's wife said in counseling that she'd rather have a car accident than find out Marcus was still seeing Sadie.

"What kind of car accident?" Sadie asked.

"I don't know," Marcus said impatiently. He was always in a bad mood after counseling. "She might have meant a fatal car accident or she might have meant a disfiguring car accident or she might have meant a fender bender. I also don't know where she figures on it happening or whether our insurance premiums would go up."

This bothered Sadie all day, being compared to a car accident.

As she and Roderick lay in bed that night, it was still on Sadie's mind.

"What would be worse—" she began, but her nerve failed her.

"Worse than what?" Roderick asked. He was reading *The Economist*.

Sadie fingered the lace on the edge of her nightgown. "Just— what would—what is a very bad thing you could imagine happening?"

"Egypt electing a Muslim Brotherhood president," Roderick said without hesitating. "That would be a disaster."

It was actually just as reassuring as anything he might have said if he'd known what Sadie was talking about, and she rolled over suddenly and pressed herself against him.

The phrase "I want you in my mouth right now" began to worry Sadie. Or rather, the fact that she said it only during phone sex, that she could not say it innocently in some other part of her life.

No one said it at Leo's playgroup, although sometimes they said nearly the opposite—"Don't put that in your mouth!"—when a child picked up something disgusting off the floor or sidewalk. No one said it at school drop-off or pickup, and Sadie sometimes wished someone would say it, wished someone would say anything besides talking about how to get your kid to eat more fruits and vegetables. No one said it at Sadie's book club, no one said it at the pediatrician's, no one said it at the supermarket, or the pharmacy, or post office, or the dry cleaners, or the bank, or during story time at the library.

No one said it, it seemed, but Sadie.

Roderick joined a bicycling club for people over fifty. The club was going to cycle from Washington, D.C., to Portland, Maine, to raise money for the Arthritis Foundation and they trained three times a week.

The upside of this was that Roderick was out of the house more and would actually be gone for three whole weeks in May. Sadie thought surely she would be able to see Marcus then. Roderick was opposed to leaving Nelda in charge of the children overnight—he said he was afraid they'd come home and find that all the relatives had opened a bake stand in the front yard and were making empanadas in the kitchen. But Sadie trusted them. She would make it work.

The downside of the cycle club was that now on Monday, Wednesday, and Thursday evenings, Sadie's kitchen was filled with sweaty gray-haired men in cycling shorts, filling their water bottles and talking about cog freewheel removal. They all had a special biking app on their iPhones that recorded their times and distances, and reminded Sadie of when the children were babies and she used to talk about how many ounces of formula they'd drunk. Frequently Nelda and her relatives were still in the kitchen, too, because although Nelda's workday officially ended at five o'clock, they took no more notice of that than they did of any other time.

This made a lot of people for Sadie to step around as she made spaghetti for Leo and Rufus, a lot of voices to talk over when it was time to persuade the boys to go to bed. And although when Sadie was younger, she had hoped someday to have a house that was a place where people liked to gather, a hub of social activity, she had had something else in mind. She hadn't meant this.

Marcus's wife went on a business retreat for her company, so Sadie told Roderick she was going to visit an old school friend and flew to Chicago for the weekend. She took a cab to Marcus's house and then there was the usual awkwardness of seeing him, of standing in his front hall together.

Sadie felt like a schoolgirl, because despite all their hundreds of hours of phone sex and conversation, she and Marcus had spent only a limited time in each other's physical presence. Sadie supposed that time-wise, they were actually only on their fourth date. And she felt like a hooker, because, let's not mess around, they were here to have sex and lots of it. (Always at this point

Sadie secretly wanted to start discussing whether an hour was an hour or fifty minutes.) And because Sadie couldn't wait for the sex, she also felt like a man, or how she supposed a man went around feeling pretty much all the time.

And then she and Marcus were kissing, and his tongue was in her mouth and her hands were in his hair, and then for a little while, although not nearly long enough, Sadie felt like herself.

Marcus's wife called every few hours, apparently to reassure herself that if Marcus was home then he wasn't out somewhere, up to no good. Of course, Marcus was in and up to no good, but his wife didn't know that. Sadie and Marcus were invariably in bed when she called (because they spent all their time together in bed) and sometimes while he talked to his wife, Marcus would run his hand absently over Sadie's naked hip, like an executive fiddling with a coffee cup.

The third time his wife called, Sadie slipped on a T-shirt and walked very quietly to the bathroom and sat on the edge of the bathtub, her bare feet on the cold tiles. She seldom thought about Marcus's wife, even while staying in her house, except for noticing that this house smelled like furniture polish and lavender while Sadie's own house always seemed to smell like a garlicky Labrador. But now, as the cold worked its way up Sadie's legs, she thought of Marcus's wife, warm and dry and snug in her hotel room, with no idea that the very air she moved through was swarming with hidden dangers, that she might as well be driving home after the bars closed on New Year's Eve in a car with broken headlights and balding tires.

· ·

Of course, Sadie called Roderick from Chicago, too.

She called and he told her that he'd cycled seventy-four miles and could have gone a hundred but his bike threw its chain in Silver Spring.

"Oh," Sadie said. "Be sure to pay Nelda extra for working on the weekend."

"What about all these other people?" Roderick asked. "Do I pay them, too?"

"No," Sadie said. "They just show up."

She asked if she could speak to Rufus, and Roderick set the phone down and in the background she could hear Rufus say, "I can't stop now!" Roderick came back and said that she couldn't speak to Rufus because he was in the middle of a Tinkertoy construction. He said she couldn't speak to Leo because he was asleep with his head on the kitchen table next to a bowl of rice. He said she couldn't speak to the dog because the dog had escaped from the backyard and run away, but that some nice woman called to say she'd found him and a bunch of Nelda's relatives had gone off to collect him an hour ago.

"But you can speak to me," Roderick said.

"Well, yes," Sadie said.

In the cab on the way to the airport on Sunday, Sadie suddenly caught her breath. She didn't know where her underpants were. Not the underpants she was *wearing*, obviously; she knew where those were. But the pair she'd been wearing when she arrived at Marcus's house. The ones he had pulled off as he pressed her against the kitchen counter. She could remember them dangling from her ankle briefly and then she'd kicked them off. But where had they gone from there? She had meant to pick them up—had reminded herself—but had she? Or were they now lying in Marcus's recycling bin or fruit bowl?

She called him as soon as the cab dropped her off. "Don't freak out," she said. "But it seems I may have left a pair of underpants at your house."

"Underpants?" Marcus said. It sounded like he'd never heard the word before but Sadie knew it was just the early stages of shock.

"Yes," she said slowly. "In the kitchen somewhere, I think."

"Underpants?" Marcus said again.

They seemed to be stuck.

"Go look," she said. "And call me back if you find them."

Her mouth was dry and she could feel her pulse thudding in her ears. She checked all the pockets of her purse and stopped to open her suitcase and paw through it frantically on the sidewalk, but her underpants weren't there.

Marcus didn't call back, and the fact that Sadie checked her phone a hundred times—in line at security, rushing through the terminal, waiting at the gate—failed to summon him.

She boarded the plane and the flight attendant came through with little foil packets of peanuts. Sadie leaned down to put hers in her purse to give to Rufus later, and there in the outside pocket, completely flattened, were her black lace panties. She could see them now, in the harsh light of the plane.

Suddenly it was not blood flowing through Sadie's veins, but honey: slow and sweet and delicious.

She pulled out her phone and called Marcus.

"Guess what?" she said happily. "I found my underpants!"

The man sitting next to Sadie was about to eat a peanut and he appeared to inhale it when she spoke. He began coughing.

"Marcus?" she said. "Did you hear me?"

"Yes," he said. "I heard you."

"Well, isn't that great?" Sadie said. The man next to her was still coughing and she had to stifle the impulse to snap at him to be quiet.

"Look," Marcus said. "I don't think I can keep doing this. This last hour has been terrible. I thought I was going to have a heart attack."

"I know——" Sadie began but he cut her off.

"I can't go through my wife finding out again," Marcus said. "Even the therapist says we'd never come back from that."

The therapist! Sadie could not believe he was quoting the therapist, to her of all people. It felt like a small animal with sharp claws was digging at her chest.

"Marcus——" she began desperately, but suddenly the flight attendant was standing beside her.

"You have to turn your phone off now," she said, smiling an iron-hard smile.

Sadie was about to protest when she realized Marcus was no longer there.

She dropped the hand holding her phone to her lap. The screen was dark.

"You have to turn it off, not just stop talking on it," the flight attendant said. Then she looked past Sadie to the man next to her. "Are you okay, sir? You're not allergic to peanuts, are you?"

Sadie turned to look at him. He was a businessman in a rumpled blue suit, still coughing. He shook his head at the flight attendant and she moved on, but Sadie kept looking at him. His skin was flushed and his eyes were damp and the muscles of his face were spasming slightly, as though he were in pain.

Sadie was sure she looked exactly the same way.

· ·

Sadie got out of the taxi in front of her house and started up the walk. The front door banged open, and the dog burst out, with a smear of green paint along his side. Roderick came out, too, in his cycling clothes, and the boys followed, with Nelda behind them, wiping her hands on a towel.

Sadie tried to smile, wishing she had time to catch her breath before they all demanded something from her.

Leo launched himself from the top porch step into Sadie's arms with a fervor usually reserved for military homecomings. He smelled like syrup and his hands were sticky in her hair.

Sadie staggered slightly under the weight of him and kissed the top of his head.

"I *missed* you," he said accusingly, not loosening his grip.

"I missed you, too," she said.

"There was a military coup in Mali," Roderick said, and Rufus, who loved to be the bearer of bad news, almost shouted, "Nelda's going back to the Philippines for six months!"

She looked at Nelda, who nodded expressionlessly, like a prison guard, or a housekeeper.

Sadie was so tired her hands shook and tears trembled on the edge of her lower eyelids, like the row of glass beads on a shower curtain. She bowed her head over Leo's blond one. Not many more years before Leo would be embarrassed to declare his love for her like this. Nelda was leaving. The relatives would disperse, never to be seen again. Roderick was going away for three weeks, the first cycling trip of many, she was sure. The thought of Marcus was like a stone in her throat, making it hard to swallow. This is how it was going to be from here on out, she realized suddenly, nothing but a long series of partings, each one ripping at the fabric of her: good-bye, and good-bye, and good-bye.

Acknowledgments

First, thank you to Kim Witherspoon and Allison Hunter. I am lucky enough to have the best agents on the face of this or any other planet. It's true.

Special thanks to my editor, Jenny Jackson, for making me better when she could have just made me happy, for taking up permanent residence in my head, and for justifying all my bad habits. Felicity Rubenstein, Clare Reihill, and Lettice Franklin, thanks for everything, but especially for keeping me in mind.

Thanks to all the unpaid editors who gave so generously of their insights: Cecile Koster, Samir Rawas Sarayji, Sofia Borgstein, Vanessa Deij, Joel Kuntonen, Patrick Walczy, Cathy Cruise, Jim Ohlson, David Kidd, Nancy Woodruff, Kathryn Ivers, Kara Parmelee, Karen Rile, Sascha Radetsky, Elizabeth Cohen, and especially Bill Roorbach. I know there is never enough time in the day (to say nothing of energy in the reader), but you all found time and energy for me.

Thanks to the editors who first picked these stories out of slush and published them: Roger Angell, James D'Agostino, Olga Zilberbourg, Julia Patt, C. Michael Curtis, James Reed, Elizabeth McKenzie, Ronald Spatz, and Ladette Randolph. I don't know how you found them, but I'm unbelievably glad you did.

Thanks to Ingrid Michaelson, for her generosity and inspiration.

For friendship beyond measure, thanks to Leila Barbaro, Jojo Harter, Kitty Lei Harter, Jessica Hörnell, and Jennifer Richardson Merlis. I will keep my promise not to tell which characters and events were inspired by you — just know that you are all in here and the book is immeasurably better because of it. My life is better because of it, too.

Thanks to my father, Richard Heiny, without whom none of this (but especially the jokes about scientifically-minded people) would have been possible. To James McCredie and Alex Muir Wood, who make my world so much richer and funnier than it would have been otherwise. To my brother, Christopher Heiny, for a lifetime of technical support. To Angus McCredie and Hector McCredie, for so patiently helping me figure out this mothering business. And most of all, to my husband, Ian McCredie, who gave up everything just to be with me.

A Note on the Type

The text of this book was set in a typeface named Perpetua, designed by the British artist Eric Gill (1882–1940) and cut by the Monotype Corporation of London in 1928–30.

Designed by Betty Lew